A New Beginning

A New Beginning

Mary Torbenson

Copyright © 2009 by Mary Torbenson.

Library of Congress Control Number:	2009911112
ISBN: Hardcover	978-1-4415-9156-2
Softcover	978-1-4415-9155-5

All rights reserved. No part of this book may be reproduced or transmitted in any form or by any means, electronic or mechanical, including photocopying, recording, or by any information storage and retrieval system, without permission in writing from the copyright owner.

This is a work of fiction based on facts.

This book was printed in the United States of America.

To order additional copies of this book, contact:
Xlibris Corporation
1-888-795-4274
www.Xlibris.com
Orders@Xlibris.com
68784

DEDICATION

To my mom and dad, and their memory that lives in my heart. Many thanks to everyone who has helped me in so many ways and to those who told me stories from the past and helped fill in the gaps.

To my husband, Bob, my daughter, Jill, sisters, Edna and Ethel, for reading and rereading the manuscript, and Ethel for the beautiful poem. I would also like to express my appreciation to everyone who went out of their way to tell me how much they enjoyed the first book of the series *Uncertain Tomorrow*.

A POEM BY ETHEL BRIGGS

In the dark of the night,
She saw the red glow.
"Edna, awaken, get up,
Get dressed. We must go."

Flames licked the dark sky
As they came on the scene,
And they saw the charred rubble
Where the house had once been.

Fear gripped their hearts.
What would they find?
Would the family be safe?
Would God be so kind?

And, thankfully, there
In their nightcloths, they were.
Sam and Dora—the girls.
"Thanks be to God" was her prayer.

All was gone, all was lost,
Save an old rocking chair.
Could they rise once again?
Or give up in despair?

Sam knew they could;
They'd done it before.
They were safe here together,
Did they really need more?

PROLOGUE

Mary, the youngest of Sam and Dora's girls and the author of this book . . . I wish I'd lived through the times when this book and its predecessor, *Uncertain Tomorrow*, were written about. I wish I'd been there when they farmed or lived in Bowbells, North Dakota, where some of the stories took place.

I wish I had lived in Denmark when a German soldier proved to be good rather than bad. I wish I had been there to comfort my sisters and parents when their house burned to the ground, destroying everything. The book with Dad's many drawings and plans, their clothes, shoes, mother's wedding ring, the dressers Dad had built for my sisters, and all of their money—gone—and they had no insurance. Even then I'd like to have seen my dad wearing the black paten leather shoes given to him by his brother Anton after the fire and how he must have looked with the red plaid shirt with the sleeves torn off at the elbows and patched-up pants that were too short, when he'd laugh and give a little dance at times when he probably felt like crying. I even wish I'd been there when Mom had to sift the weevils from the flour she'd gotten from the mill during the Great Depression or watched my sisters, Luella and Edna, when the cattle had to be herded to market, with Edna riding on horseback and receiving only fifteen dollars a head from the government. But I'm grateful to have heard the stories and privileged to have written it all down.

Sam was a master carpenter as well as a farmer, and Dora possessed both the will and the tenacity of her parents. But would it be enough to withstand the loss of everything they worked so hard for? Together they face the tragedy and triumph of life on the Dakota Plains. They and their girls are a family knit together through good times and bad.

A NEW BEGINNING

Mary wondered about the uncertainty of tomorrow, but right now, she wondered if they would ever be warm again. Winter on the North Dakota Plains was so cold.

The shack was impossible to keep warm with the small parlor stove and, even worse, for the lack of fuel to feed it. The wood was saved to be burned mostly at night and to prepare their meager meals. a tin box oven was mounted to the stovepipe, only large enough to bake a single loaf of bread.

Mary Adamson sat just inside the wooden slat door of the small homestead shack, twisting the long coarse slew grass into tight knots to burn. Her hands were bleeding, staining the socks she'd pulled on with spots of red. Her hands hurt with every twist, and she wondered why she hadn't put her hands inside the socks to begin with instead of letting them be cut by the sharp edges of the grass? The cold must be dulling her senses.

The shack, barely twelve feet in any direction, was built hurriedly once the train brought them to the northern part of North Dakota from Iowa. It had been only September, but already the ground was frozen, and there'd been no time to waste. So leaving the two youngest—Emil, five, and Dora, two and a half—at the immigrant shack with Mary Inga to keep watch over their belongings. John and Mary Adamson and their son Peter loaded the meager pile of lumber from a pigsty and corncrib torn down in Iowa and the small can of straightened nails into the wagon to take out to the homestead. It'd taken them three days, returning to the immigrant shack each evening, where Mary Inga had supper waiting.

Andrew Peterson, Jebbe and Thea Skow, and the Olsons had come with them from Iowa and had chosen land adjacent to John and Mary, east of the small town of Bowbells.

A new beginning was not new to them, only the place, time, and circumstance. Only a few years earlier, John and Mary Adamson with their three young children and Mary's sister Thea had left their beloved Denmark for America, hoping that the American climate would cure their little Dora Amelia Tora and also because of the growing unrest in southern Denmark already under German rule and aggression.

Expecting John to work at his American uncle's farm in Iowa, they had been expectant of a good life in America.

Though the voyage, possibly the salt air, had seemed to help little Dora, it had proven too much for John. His inclination toward a weak stomach and the continual rocking of the ship caused him to have seasickness the whole voyage, leaving him in a deplorably weakened condition. So when the uncle in Iowa took one look at him, a wife heavy with child, and a sickly little girl, along with young Peter, Mary Inga, and Thea Knutson, he apparently, without remorse, turned them away.

It had been a terrible time, but in the midst of it all, Andrew Peterson—a man who worked for the uncle—came to their rescue, finding them shelter and bringing them food and a little Irish angel of mercy named Rose. Yet a week later, little Dora Amelia Tora died. In their grief, the family, without means and John too weak to work, had to carry on.

But it was now here on the homestead land that John had chosen that they were fulfilling a dream of owning their own land. John and Mary and their growing family, Peter, Mary Inga, Emil, and little Dora, named for their Dora Amelia Tora who lay buried in Iowa. And in the late spring, there would be still another.

Mary Inga worked the knitting needles in and out as a sock took shape. Putting the work in her lap, she looked up. "*Mor*, how long before Christmas?"

"Soon. Why do you ask?"

"I want to make Dory a yarn doll."

"*Nei*! We mustn't waste the yarn, but you can make a small cloth doll with yarn hair from scraps and stitch the eyes, nose, and mouth. Make a smiling face! Dory will like that."

"Can I start it now while she is napping?"

"*Ja*, if you like."

Mary Inga was looking through a small bundle of scraps to decide which to use for the doll when the door burst open, letting in a blast of frigid air as her father and brother Pete came in. Pushing the door closed against the wind, they held out their hands to the heat from the fire.

Mary reached to push the coffee pot to the hottest spot on the stove and said, "You have been gone a long time. Was Thea and the children well?"

"Ja, they were well." John pointed to the roll of felt he'd brought in. "Jebbe gave me the last of his felt. They have a double thickness on the inside walls of their shack. I think there will be enough for at least one layer on ours. It will help to keep out some of the cold."

John poured himself a cup of coffee and held his hands around the warmth of the cup for a moment before taking a sip. He said, "Sometimes I wish I would have built a Soddy. At least we would be warm now. I shouldn't have been so pig headed."

"John, you know how they smell. The smell of the earth and cooking . . . oh my, you couldn't have stood it."

"Ja, but some soddies smell better than others."

"Well, some are cleaner than others but even so . . ."

"I just hope this tar paper helps us to be warmer." And he shivered and looked over at Emil and Dora huddled under the quilts on the bed and Mary Inga dressed in her warmest of clothing as she sat sewing upon the stool.

Mary was quick to say, "And we'll pray for more snow to pack against the outside."

"I think we'll have snow soon enough from the looks of the sky." It hadn't snowed since the last week in November, and a few days of milder temperatures had melted the snow they'd packed against the shack as insulation against the cold and the ever-present wind.

Mary hadn't thought she would ever wish for snow, and now they prayed for it, glad for even a flurry that might mean a sign of more snow to come. If only they could bury their little shack in snow until spring.

Mary glanced up from her work and asked, "There was no mail?"

"*Nei*! Jebbe went to town just yesterday and there was none."

Mary bit her lip. "I cannot understand why no one has written. Do you suppose there is something wrong, something they don't want to tell us?"

"You worry too much," said John. "We'll have a letter soon."

Mary knew he was right, but she couldn't help but wonder though goodness knows there were plenty of other things to worry about.

"Supper will be ready as soon as you and Pete finish the chores," she said as she put the pile of grass that lay in her lap to one side, but as she did, John saw the blood-stained socks on her hands.

"Mary, what have you done to your hands? Take off those socks and let me see."

When she pulled her hands free of the socks, John took them into his own and said, "What have you done? Do you want an infection? How did this happen?"

Mary was close to tears. "I know, I know, I was so foolish. I should have put my hands in the socks before I started, but I didn't think about the grass cutting my hands until it did. But twisting it into knots is the only way to keep it burning longer. Otherwise, it just flares up in the flames and is gone in seconds. I'll wrap them in cloth and get supper on."

John shook his head. "I'll take the team in the morning to find wood somewhere. I don't want to go far, but I will if I have to." With that, he turned toward the door and motioned for Pete to follow, but Pete hesitated a moment and said, "Mor, there are a few small trees left by the creek. I'll cut them for the fire before we go in the morning."

Mary smiled. "Ja, that would be good." But she knew they were but spindly cottonwood and not much more than brush and would not last much longer than the slew grass. She'd known they were there by the creek, left after cutting the trees, but somehow the thought of them brought some measure of comfort, just knowing they were there if all else was gone.

Dora woke from her nap, and she and Emil began playing string games with Mary Inga and acting silly while their sister tried to keep them serious about the game.

Mary turned her attention toward supper. There were no choices to make because their dwindling food supply was simple: a scant two layers of salt pork in the bottom of the crock, a sack of frozen potatoes, flour, lard, a little sugar to save for Christmas, salt, and whatever milk the cow gave and whatever was left after the hogs were fed.

The precious rutabagas had frozen and turned to mush, and no matter what she'd done to make them palatable, it was of no use, so John threw them to the hogs. Grunting and squealing, they tried to push one another away with their snouts, each afraid they would not get their share of the rutabagas.

The family longed for a juicy sausage or a bite of flaky pastry or, better yet, a taste of herring and some Danish cheese.

Morning broke as a clear, sunny, but very cold day; and John would have to go to the creek to break a hole in the ice so the livestock could drink and carry water to the pigs. Pete was well ahead of him with the ax lying over his shoulder as he headed for two small trees that looked more like brush.

The ice in the creek had turned out to be so thick that only a very small stream ran beneath it, so John had had no choice but to chop chunks of ice to melt over the stove for the pigs. "A few more days like this and we'll have to melt ice to water all of the livestock and ourselves," he said as he sat by the table with a cup of watered-down coffee while Mary spread lard between the cut halves of four biscuits and wrapped them in a cloth for John and Pete to take along for their trip to find wood. "Don't go far, John! It's too cold to be out for long."

"Don't worry. Andrew told me of a place where he'd gotten some good fire wood, but we need to get going. We'll milk when we get home." But it was after dark before Mary heard the bells on the horses' harness, and she had already milked and fed the livestock and melted ice throughout the day for water.

The wagon was loaded with logs, and while John unhitched the horses and led them to the barn, Mary walked her half-frozen son inside to the warmth of the fire. The logs would wait until the next day to be sawed in lengths and split, but just the sight of them made her heart beat faster.

The next evening, John told her of his plan to butcher a hog as soon as the wood was split. She knew it wouldn't be easy to ready the meat in such small quarters as their little shack, but they had no choice. She might even try a few rolls of sausage, and she thought of the small pouch of seasonings tucked away inside the America trunk next to her journal. Her journal, she would take it out after everyone was asleep and write about their homestead on the North Dakota Prairie and about their dreams for tomorrow.

The day to butcher came, and the straw ticks were piled on top of one another in a corner, as they were every morning to make room to walk about, and the table was set in the center of the small room. Emil and Dora were told to play on the bed in the corner to be out of the way while John brought first one part of the hog to be cut up and then another and while Mary sawed the bone and sliced the meat, Mary Inga layered it in a crock, salting each layer as she went. Scalding the hog had been next to impossible without a barrel big enough to dip it in, but with Jebbe's help, they had managed to scrape most of the stiff coarse hair from the carcass. However, until the meat from that hog was all eaten, they would find the stiff hairs on their plates.

Scraping and washing the hog's intestines for sausage casing proved to be impractical, so for them, Mary seasoned the meat John ground and shaped it into patties to be fried. Even the blood saved for blood sausage was made into a pudding laced with ground fat and fried.

It was two days before Christmas when a letter arrived from Denmark, and Mary brushed the flour from her hands as John handed her the envelope. But before she had a chance to get it opened, first one and then another said, "Read it, Mor. Read it out loud."

Unfolding the letter she read:

> My dears,
>
> My hope is that you get this post before it is Christmas, but if not, we all send you a Christmas greeting. We received your letter about your new home on the North Dakota Prairie. We pray you are well and wish we could see all of you, and I am sure we will one day. Frederick and Elsie now have two sons, and Heinrick and Helga have one daughter. Lana has one son and a daughter, and Anna now has one boy and two girls. Chrisian has not yet married. We have not seen the captain in some time, but we have heard that your friend Bjorn is in the German Army as are your brothers, Frederick and Heinrick. I am sorry to write you such sad news, but your brothers are well, and we see them often.
>
> Thea, I have seen your daughter recently. She was with a young woman who I believe is her half sister. I spoke to her, and she smiled and acknowledged my greeting, but

the young woman hurried her away. Dorthea resembles you greatly and appeared to be strong and healthy, so at least you can rest assured that she is being well taken care of. I will send the address when I get it so you can write to her.

Your *tanta,* Dorthea

Mary faltered over the words, trying to keep her composure as she read the news about her brothers and Thea's daughter, the baby who'd been taken from her.

John stepped to Mary's side and laid a hand on her shoulder, and she turned into his embrace and cried softly as he held her close against his chest and whispered, "My girl, your brothers will be all right. You shall see!"

Lifting her face to him and wiping away the tears, she said, "Ja, I know!" and quickly turned her attention to little Dora who was crying at her mother's distress.

That night, as they lay in the darkness, Mary whispered, "I hate to show the letter to Thea. You know how she'll react, and I want to spare her the anguish of a fresh reminder that she had to leave her baby in Denmark, but we are invited to spend Christmas Eve with them. I think I'll wait to show her the letter after Christmas."

John answered simply, "Ja!"

Over the years since they'd come to America, Thea had more and more pushed the baby she'd borne and left behind from her thoughts, thoughts that were too painful to bear. She'd always blamed herself for not stealing her child away from the man who'd fathered her.

Snow began to fall early on Christmas Eve morning as Pete carried a small stickery buffalo brush toward the shack. The snow grew heavier as he walked until at times he lost sight of the shack. He heard his father call, and he followed the sound of his voice and answered, "Coming, Far!" At the door, he shook the snow from the brush before taking it inside.

"What have you there?" John scowled.

"A Christmas tree!" Pete beamed.

Mary took the brush from him and held it at arm's length. "A fine tree." And looking at John, she said, "It will be beautiful." After placing the root in an empty lard pail, she set it on the table and opened the lid of the America trunk. There, beneath the journal and the securely wrapped porcelain dogs, laid a silver star that she placed at the top of the Christmas tree.

John merely grumbled, "Ja." But she saw a twinkle in his eye.

Mary Inga had already cut small squares from the most colorful scrapes of cloth and ran a thread through the middle and pulled it tight to make small bows for the tree, and once they were placed on its branches, it brightened the whole room.

By the afternoon, it was clear that going to the Skows was impossible. Snow had drifted from the wind into banks against the shack and animal shelter and the outhouse was nearly lost from sight.

They were disappointed, but soon, Mary had supper started, adding the squash she had saved and cared for against the cold and had prepared to take to Thea. Sprinkling it with sugar and a chunk of butter, she set it on the table to eat with their supper.

With heads bowed, John prayed, "Father, we thank thee for your bountiful gifts, and we pray for family and friends and especially for those in our homeland. And Lord help us to stay warm. Amen."

It was still storming as John and Pete went to feed the animals and milk the cow, giving the animals an extra portion, as was John's custom at Christmas even though the hay they'd been forced to buy was dwindling, as was the feed grain they'd brought from Iowa. Before they went back into the falling snow, John dug his hand into the grain. And then closing the barn door behind them, he sprinkled the grain on a sheltered board for the birds, an age-old custom in Denmark.

In other years, he had saved small bundles of wheat or oats tied with string and placed on top of fence posts while the family scrubbed clean and dressed in their best watched.

Perhaps the next year the tradition could be resumed, but for now, this would have to do.

Stomping the snow from their boots, John and Pete hung their coats on the pegs by the door and sniffed as John said, "Something smells mighty good." And on the table, he saw small bowls of *romagrout, a* Danish pudding and a plate of cookies. But before they ate the delicacies, they were seated, and John offered up a prayer as the family bowed their heads. Mary Inga passed about the gifts she and her mother had made: a pair of warm wool socks for her Pa and Pete, and mittens for Emil. She saved Dora's for last and watched the excitement on her small face when she saw the smiling rag doll. Mary had knit Mary Inga a new pair of mittens, and Mary Inga had embroidered a handkerchief for her mother. The family was seated on the log stools John had made and given to them earlier, when Pete and Emil stood up and went to the bed in the corner where all of the straw ticks were stacked until bedtime when they were laid on the floor and covered with quilts. They each reached in beneath the bed and withdrew a parcel, which they unwrapped and handed the gifts they had made to their family.

Pete handed his father a small stick he had smoothed and polished. "This is to clean the bowl of your pipe."

John said, "*Danker*, I surely needed this."

And then to his mother a long-handled stirring stick. "You can use this when you make soap."

"Ya, this is good. *Danker.*"

Pete handed his sisters a carved wooden button with a string through the holes and demonstrated how to use it as he explained, "Hold the ends of the string and spin it around with one hand, and then pull both ends, and it will sing." Mary Inga smiled and Dora's face lit up.

Mil had saved brightly colored leaves from the fall and pasted on to a thin piece of wood for the whole family. He handed it to his mother, and she said, "Ah, now I know why you wanted the spoon of flour, to make paste! It is very beautiful." Emil beamed.

This was the first of many Christmases on the plains of North Dakota, and without doubt, the most memorable in its beautiful simplicity.

* * *

The remainder of the winter went on with one snowstorm after another, and all the time, the child Mary carried grew heavier and the hunger for potatoes and other vegetables grew greater. They prayed each day for the strength for yet another day.

It was nearing the end of April when John saw the first crocus poking through the melting snow and knew that spring had really arrived. Plucking it, he handed it to Pete. "Here, take this to your mother." And when Mary saw it, she burst into a flood of joyful tears.

A week later, the heifer had a little bull calf, and by the first of May, John was able to put the plow to a spot of ground near the homestead shack. Before long, a garden spot was ready for the disk, going back and forth to break up the big clods before he could use the drag to smooth that first patch of virgin prairie for a garden. Making rows in the new ground meant pulling and shaking the clods not broken up by the machinery, but at last, it was done and the rows made. Even Emil and little Dora had helped shake the clods, and now it was time to plant. A few of the larger seeds like corn were given to Emil, who placed them just so in the furrow before Dora's small hands brushed the dirt over them.

That evening, John and Mary sat outside on a bench near the door. There was a slight breeze sending the sweet smell of the buffalo brush in bloom, and they smiled at one another. They were silent; it had been a good day.

The next morning, John hitched the team to the plow and dragged it to where he would begin breaking the first eighty acres and setting the plow in place. With the reins looped about his neck, he hollered, "Oop!" and the team danced in place and with heads lowered, lurched forward, pulling the plow as it dug deep into the heavy soil, laying over the sod in rows. It was the beginning of months of hard work to prove up the first eighty acres in just three years. When he wasn't breaking sod, he was filing the plow shares or pounding them out with the heavy sledge. It was while working the soil that he was glad there were so few rocks. Mary's words, before he'd come to North Dakota last spring to find land for a homestead, still haunted him.

She'd said, "Be sure there is water at hand until we can dig a well and look to the soil, no rocks or clay." And he smiled.

The homestead shack seemed to grow smaller by the day though they could now be out of doors much of the time, but with another child soon to be born, it was decided that an addition to the shack was needed, and John would take the wagon into Bowbells to buy lumber. Mary wished she could ask him to add a few potatoes to the list but knew how their meager savings were dwindling. They would have potatoes once the potato vines bloomed and faded, but that seemed like forever.

New spring grass was coming up everywhere, so the animals no longer needed hay, and there was plenty of milk for the pigs now that Agnes the cow had dropped a fine little heifer calf, and the heifer that came with them from Iowa, which Emil named Bess, had proven to be a good cow as well. Once her calf was weaned and put to the pail, Mary was able to milk her easily, and her milk was rich and plentiful.

John had built a box to set in the creek to keep the milk and butter cool. And because there was enough milk, Mary asked, "Could you make a cheese form? We can spare enough milk for a brick of cheese."

John smiled, "Ya, sure! Cheese sounds mighty good. It's been quite a time since we've had any."

Lining the mold with cheesecloth a few days later, Mary filled it to the brim with curd, and pressing out the whey, she put it up on the roof of the shack to cure in the sun. The job of climbing to the roof to grease the top of it with butter several times a day was given to Mary Inga until she passed the job on to Emil.

The middle of June turned hot, so Mary and Mary Inga sat outside to shell peas from the garden. They were having fresh vegetables every day now, and they were grateful for the provision of good weather with just enough rain. God had heard their prayers.

It was on such a day that Mary suddenly stiffened, feeling the first pain of labor. By afternoon, it was plain that it would not be long. A new baby would join the Adamson family soon.

Calling Mary Inga who was weeding the garden, she said, "Mary, will you ask Pete to go for Thea right away? It's nearly time."

"Yes, Mor," she answered as she ran to the field where Pete was helping their father.

After the baby girl was born, Thea wrapped her in a small blanket and opened the outside door where the family waited. The baby was named Elsie Hannah, but when Dora said her name, it sounded more like Ella. And so it was Ella. The name she would go by from then on. It was June 17, 1899.

The days were full with so many things to do, and baby Ella's birth had been a difficult one, as Mary had bled profusely, leaving her in a weakened condition, but there was still work to be done.

Concern was etched on John's face when he'd come in from the field to find Mary, her face pale with beads of sweat on her forehead and little wisps of brown hair damp and curled about her face. But he said nothing until one day, he found her in the garden, leaning against a post with her eyes closed.

"Mary, are you sick? What is wrong?"

"Nei! I am fine. Do you want something to eat?"

"Mary, you are not fine. Why isn't Mary Inga helping you? And Emil . . . he is big enough to help."

"Oh, John, the children help both of us as much as they can. Mary is right now preparing the fat to make soap. And Emil is watching after Dora and Ella, and of course Pete is helping you in the field."

"Ja, I know, but you are so pale, and what is this you are doing?" He looked toward a shovel and a hole in the ground.

"A root cellar. I want it big enough and deep enough so we can walk down into it. I thought we could lay boards over the top and dig out steps to get into it."

"And you thought you could do this by yourself? I'll send Pete to help you." John knew better than to try to discourage her, but as he turned to walk away, he said. "I'll build walls and put a roof over and layer it with sod." He turned to grin at her, and she grinned back.

The trips into town were few since they required both time and money of which they had little, but when Andrew came to visit, he brought news of a celebration in Bowbells on the Fourth of July. The Adamsons had been in America long enough to be acquainted with some of the country's customs, and the Fourth of July was a date highly celebrated. It was the anniversary of the signing of the Declaration of Independence, when the United States of America declared independence from English rule.

It was decided that the family would go to town for the celebration, so that morning, everyone was dressed in their very best. But moments before they were to go, Emil came dragging Dora from behind the shack, her dress covered in mud and her stockings sagging.

"Dora Amelia! Look at you, you are a mess," John shouted.

But when she began to cry, rubbing her eyes with her dirty hands, Mary went to her side and led her to a water bucket sitting beside the door of the shack. Her dress and stockings had to be changed, and since the dress she wore was the only good one she had, she had to wear a dress with a mended tear.

People were busy setting up tables in the shade beneath some trees at the end of the street when they arrived.

Mary had wanted to bake buns for the occasion, but with only the small stovepipe oven, it was not practical. So instead, she made sweet-and-sour cabbage but without the apple, still it tasted good. She fried the quail Pete had snared and added it to the basket along with a good chunk of butter and one of cheese.

The women milling about the tables smiled as they came up, and as John set the basket, he was carrying on the table. He was glad to see that the trees lent an amount of shade on such a hot day. And then he said, "I see the Skows, I'll go talk to Jebbe while you women get dinner on." He spoke in German, the more familiar language, since it was the language they were forced to use in the old country since their part of Denmark was under German rule. It had been their intent to speak Dane until they mastered the English language, but speaking German was easier.

Thea called, "Mary!" as she hurried up, leading Crist and little Walter by the hand. "Isn't this just wonderful? It's been so long since we have been to a festivity." And she set a basket of freshly baked buns on the table. Jebbe had bought a cook stove with an oven soon after they arrived in Dakota, and Mary couldn't help but be a little envious. Greeting Thea, she said, "Ja! It is grand, and those buns look so good."

Just then, Mrs. Olson walked toward them, carrying a big bowl of creamed potatoes and setting them down she said, "*Godag!*" in Norwegian. Then turning toward a group of other women standing near, she said, "Good day!" in English. And turning her face to Mary and Thea, she looked at them soberly and nodded her head ever so slightly, indicating they should follow her example, and they did with great effort. But then a woman walked up to them and took one of each of their hands in hers and said in Danish. "It is good to meet you. My name is Anne Sorensen."

Once Mary and Thea introduced themselves and explained why they had spoken in German, they were introduced to other homesteaders' wives, and the festivities began. There were two different speakers, and both spoke only English, so they understood very little of what was being said, but John suspected their speech was a campaign for some position in government.

The day ended with a stop at the mercantile for the few supplies they could afford, and in a box near the door were some cheeping baby chicks. When John noticed Mary looking at them with a wanting smile on her face, he asked the shop keeper their price, and when he said they were two for one penny, he asked for six. Mr. Blenkner, the storekeeper, placed them in a box and set a bag of ground chicken feed beside them. When John started to protest, Mr. Blenkner just waved his hand and said, "No charge."

John smiled and said, "*Mange takk*," knowing the Norwegian word for many thanks.

A spot was made using a piece of chicken wire for the baby chicks inside the barn, and Emil and Dora were put in charge of feeding them and warned not to handle them lest they die.

Mary explained, "Baby chicks are very fragile, and if you hold them, you could crush them and not even know that you are holding them too tightly. So don't pick them up until they are bigger." The very next day, one of the babies was found dead, and Emil and Dora cried. "We didn't pick it up, Mor," said Emil. "We didn't."

"I know *den lille*. Sometimes things like this happen, and we don't know why. We will pray for the other five." And as prayer would have it, the others grew and soon their yellow fuzz turned to brown feathers, and only one developed a bright red comb on its head. The others would lay eggs for the family table when they were older.

The summer was speeding by, and there were still so many things to do before winter. Mary had hoped they could dig a well before winter too, but she supposed it would have to wait for another year. It was more important to have fuel for their fire, and several of the men and boys were planning a trip to the White Earth Valley to cut and haul hardwood. What a blessing to have wood that will hold a fire overnight.

The root cellar was finished, and the hay on the homestead was cut and stacked, but it was poor hay, so John and Andrew went some distance to cut and haul several loads of good hay from a parcel of land not yet taken up for homestead. The inside walls and ceiling of the shack had been covered with wainscoting and a new thickness of tarpaper put on the outside. A deeper hole had been dug for the outhouse nearer the shack, and the Soddy built for the animals was repaired and added too. The garden harvest was better than Mary had expected, and the root cellar was full. Next year perhaps, she could put some vegetables and meat up in jars.

Another thing to finish before winter set in was the field work and butchering. And John and Pete were in the field most often before daybreak, turning the sod and disking, but the plow shear was in such bad shape that John had no choice but to buy a new one. He'd hoped to buy a new two-bottom plow to make the work go a little faster, but for now, he'd have to settle for a plow shear. In the meantime, they would finish disking up to where they'd left off the plowing.

King, the dappled gray, and Jim, with his crooked leg, were still the best team anywhere about. Sometimes Jebbe would rub it in about how nicely his team was matched and remind John about Jim's crooked leg, but all John would do was sit back in his chair, put a straw in his mouth, and grin, not saying a word. It got Jebbe riled every time.

* * *

The day John and Pete went into town for the new plow shear, Mary set up her washtub on the bench outside the door. She would leave Emil to look after Dora and Ella while she and Mary Inga went to the creek for water, but just as they started out, a man driving a team pulling a wagon came into the yard in a cloud of dust. Yelling down, he said, "Are you Mrs. Adamson?"

"Ja, I am. What is it?" She started to ask if something was wrong with John or Pete, "Had they had an accident or . . . ?"

But the man said excitedly, "It's my missus, she's having a baby. Can you help?"

Without even a second thought, she said. "Ja! Ja! Wait here while I instruct my children and get my baby. I cannot leave her. She is still nursing." And she went inside and took Ella in her arms and gathered a few diapers and things she might need, talking all the while. "Mary, tell your Pa where I have gone, and you will need to fix supper. Emil, you and Dora, mind your sister and no sassing. Do you hear?" Not even waiting for an answer, she hurried out to the man in the wagon who reached down for her hand to help her up. Seeing the children standing in the doorway, she waved and hollered, "I'll be back soon!"

The man yelled, "Hah!" to his team and snapped a rein across their backs, and away they went. Crossing near Jebbe and Thea's, Mary waved at Edward standing by their finished well, but he just looked dumbfounded at the sight and watched the wagon as it drew out of sight. Mary wondered if Edward had even known who it was who'd waved at him.

By the time they drew up to a Soddy set in a dip at the bottom of a small rise, Mary thought her bones must have jarred loose, but the baby cradled in her arms had seemed to enjoy the ride because Ella looked up at her and smiled when they climbed down.

The man hurried her into the Soddy to where his wife lay, stifling a scream with the back of her hand. The woman was wringing wet though the Soddy was comparatively cool. Turning to the man, Mary asked, "How long has she been like this? When did her labor start?"

"I don't know. She was like this when I came in from the field."

The woman looked up at her husband, "I called you, but you didn't hear me." And another pain began.

"Nei, Elsa, I didn't hear you." He sobbed and looked at Mary who had laid Ella in the waiting cradle and was folding back a sheet covering his wife. "Can you help her?" he asked.

"Ja, but you must go outside. Is there water to wash in? And I think she could use a drink as well."

"There is a pail of water outside. Should I bring it in and start a fire?"

"Nei, it's too warm for a fire. Has the water been sitting in the sun?"

"Ja!"

"Then it is warm enough. Just bring it inside if you will."

The man did as she asked and hurried back outside as his wife spoke his name, "Sven, Sven." But he didn't hear her.

"Elsa, I am Mary Adamson, and we need to get this baby born. Your husband will be just outside."

This was not Mary's first time to help with a birthing, but it was the first time she'd been snatched away by a stranger to attend to his wife.

"Elsa, your baby is ready to come, but it is tangled in the cord. I need to slip it over the baby's head, so try very hard not to push." In a minute, she'd slipped the slippery cord up and over the baby's head and said, "Now, push." And in seconds, the baby came, but it was still. Mary took the baby boy and gave it a little slap on its bottom, and then again until it let out a lusty cry, and she laid the baby across his mother's stomach while she cut the cord.

The baby's father didn't wait for an invitation once he heard the baby cry. He bound through the door to his wife's side. "Elsa, are you all right?" As soon as he saw a weak smile, he turned his attention to his son. "What will be his name?" His wife answered as she held up her hand to Mary. "Adam. We'll call him Adam after you, Mary Adamson."

Mary beamed but said, "Nei!" They knew she meant thank you.

John was home and pacing the ground outside the shack when Sven brought Mary and baby Ella home. It was almost dark, and he held up his hand to help her down before saying, "I was getting worried."

Sven swung down, and coming around the wagon, he held out his hand to John. "Manga takk. My wife would have died had it not been for your missus. My name is Sven Larson, and you must be John."

"I am glad she could help, but my children said only that she'd gone off with a man who was in a hurry and that she'd told them she would be home soon. You can understand why I was worried, especially since they didn't know who you were."

"Ja, I surely do. Forgive me. I was just so worried about my Elsa."

Sven Larson was invited in for coffee, but he wanted to get right back to his wife and son.

It was already the middle of August, and the trip to the White Earth Valley was planned for the following week, so the wood, once they cut and hauled it, would have a chance to dry out some before winter.

John was determined to finish the plowing before the trip, so it was up early to work until dark. The horses were his main concern so every hour, he let them rest. It wasn't such a bad idea for himself either. Twice during the summer, his leather truss that he wore to keep the ruptures he'd had since childhood from popping out, slipped, and he'd had to lower himself to the ground, flat on his back in order to push them in and cover them again with the belt.

The rest of the work in the field would have to wait until they returned with the logs. John wished they had another team so Pete could have stayed behind to finish the disking, but for now, it was the way it was.

One afternoon, a wagon pulled into the yard. It was Sven and Elsa Larson with their baby, Adam. Whenever Mary thought of the baby being named after her in that way, she got a lump in her throat.

"*Godag*! We wanted to show you how much Adam is growing."

"Oh, please come in."

The Larsons climbed down, and Mary seated them at the table with a cup of coffee and a plate of sliced cheese and bread and butter.

"Nei, we did not come to eat."

"I know but please . . ." and Mary pushed the plate a little closer to them.

Elsa grinned, "Ja, we are Scandinavians, aren't we?"

"Ja, that we are." Mary agreed.

Sven did not hesitate and buttered a piece of bread and covered it with two slices of cheese/ He buttered another slice of bread to put on top and took a large bite. After a moment of chewing and swallowing, he said, "Mighty good cheese." And he went on eating until he turned to his wife. "Elsa, ask Mrs. Adamson to show you how to make this fine cheese."

"Ja!" and turning to Mary, she asked, "Will you?"

"Ja, I will! I can tell you now." Mary took an empty form and rummaging for a piece of cheesecloth to line it she told Elsa how to ready the curd and proceed with the curing. Then, smiling, she said, "There. That is all there is to it. Take this form and this bit of cheesecloth."

John and Pete were gone for two days to the White Earth Valley for hardwood, and once they returned, the logs were cut into stove-length pieces. John took the team to the field, and Pete was left to split the wood. After splitting a pile, he called. "Emil, come stack the wood while I split."

As Emil came running with Dora right behind him, he beamed at being told to do such an important job as stacking wood, but an hour later as the stack grew, Pete complained about his stacking. Emil was near tears. It was Dora who threw the piece of wood she was carrying to the ground and put her hands on her hips and held her chin up and said to Pete, "Mil is a good tacker."

"Okay, okay, but the stack has to be taller, and you're too short. Go on, I'll do it myself." As Pete swung the ax at another piece of wood, Dora pulled at Emil's arm and led him away.

A day of celebration in Bowbells was set for the first day of October—a tradition for Scandinavians and Germans alike, October Fest. This is when the harvest was over and a time of rest and the giving of thanks for the bounties of the summer's crops were heralded. There would be food, games, music, and dancing. Everyone could hardly wait.

There was just one thing Mary kept thinking of—a well. But she'd all but given up hope of having one that year because soon, the ground would be too frozen and hard to dig. When Sven and Elsa and baby Adam had been there, Mary had mentioned not having a well, and to everyone's surprise, just a few days before the October Fest, Sven came by. Seated next to him was Ole Hanson, the man John and the others had met when they came to find their homestead land. Sven hollered down, "We come to dig your well."

John looked dumbfounded. "Our well?"

"Ja, your well." And before he could say another word, they climbed from the wagon.

Ole Hanson asked, "Do you know where you want it?"

"Nei, I really don't know where to find water or how deep it is." John knew he must sound like an idiot, but he'd never been faced with digging a well before.

Ole went to the back of the wagon and reached for a dry V-shaped tree branch and held it up. "We'll have the spot to dig in no time." And he began walking in all directions, holding the strange stick in front of him with the two points pointing outward. By this time, the whole family was gathered, watching the queer goings on. And then suddenly the man stopped when the points of the stick turned down toward the ground and quivered. Ole shouted "I got'er, here she is. And it can't be too deep neither from the way that stick's actin'." He jerked the thing to another position where it calmed down, and he took it back to the wagon, and he and Sven grabbed a shovel while Pete ran to the barn to get shovels for himself and his pa, and the four of them began to dig in the spot where the stick had pointed.

As they dug, John asked, "What do you call that, what you did with the stick? I've never seen the likes of it before."

"It's called witching, but it's my guess it's got nothing to do with witches."

At the end of the third day, Mary had her well, and Mrs. Ole Hanson and Elsa Larson came with their husbands that morning, bringing enough pie and *potte klub*, potato dumplings filled with chunks of pork for everyone. Mary had made a crème kake. They set up a table in the yard using boards and saw horses and covered it with a sheet.

Elsa brought a sample of her first cheese to get Mary's opinion on its taste and texture and was happy to hear that she'd passed with flying colors.

In the afternoon, Jebbe and Thea and the children came. At seeing the well, sounding half mad, Jebbe exclaimed, "When did you get a well in? Why didn't you say something, and I'd have helped you?"

John pointed to Sven and Ole before he said, "It was just as much of a surprise to me, Jebbe. These two just came and said they'd come to get my well dug, and there it is. Meet Sven Larson and Ole Hanson. Do you remember Ole from when we came in the spring to find our homesteads?"

Jebbe acknowledged his brief acquaintance with Ole and shook hands all around, but John could tell that he still resented not being asked to help.

Thea smoothed it over by reminding Jebbe of the reason they'd come. "You'll have your chance at helping. Remember, the butchering!"

"Oh yes! What about it, John? Are you going to be ready to butcher sometime in October? Mads Olson asked if I'd help them, but you and I have always done it together, and I prefer it that way. And anyway, there are the two of them, and only one of us. Of course, our boys will help but—"

John interrupted, "I was just thinking about coming by to talk with you about that. Let's watch the weather and plan a good time. We need a few colder days."

Jebbe nodded his head in agreement, "Ja, good."

The rest of the day turned out to be a prelude to the coming October Fest because Jebbe sent Edward home to bring him his violin. Only the children danced on that day, but the singing could have been heard in the next township.

The well water had to settle for a day or so to become clear, and in the meantime, John fashioned a pulley with a crank to bring the water up out of the well.

Dora seemed to be the only one of the children to be curious about the well, pulling or rolling a good-sized stump of wood to the edge of the well. She got it stood upright and climbed to the top and pulled herself up to look over the ledge into the well. She was just getting her knee up so she could sit on the ledge when her father saw her. "Dora, get down from there." He shouted as he ran toward her. But Dora, in her haste to obey him, had fallen in a heap on the ground and was crying. He picked her up and stood her in front of him and with a hand on both arms, he shook her. "Don't you ever get up there again. You could have drowned. Do you hear?"

Between sobs, she said, "Yes, Pa." And that was the end of that.

Early one morning, Andrew came with his Landrace boar, one of a litter he had in Iowa and old enough for breeding. The

Landrace breed of hog was known for its extra rib, giving it two extra pork chops. Introducing the Landrace breed to the Ruthven area of Iowa was one good deed the uncle had done when he'd sent to Denmark and had a Landrace boar shipped to him.

John's Yorkshire sow was from good stock, but it didn't have the extra rib. John and Andrew figured by mixing the bloodlines that eventually they would have the same result. But at any rate, they figured by the following year, they should each have a litter or two to sell.

It was downright chilly on the morning to butcher, but Mary set up a table in the yard just the same so they would have the extra space for cutting the meat for both families.

The fire beneath the scalding barrel was still going when the sausages were ready to boil, so the barrel was replaced with a big iron kettle, and the first of the sausages were put in to cook.

The day of the October Fest, Mary was up readying the food she would take when she stepped outside to empty a pan of water and noticed a red glow in the distance and murmured, "That is not the sun rising, it's in the wrong direction." Then realized . . . it was fire!

"John, John. Fire!"

"What? Fire?" And he was up and dressed, pulling on his boots as he headed out the door. Looking in the direction Mary pointed, he said, "I don't think it's a grass fire. I think it's Bowbells." And he started for the corral next to the barn.

"Oh dear . . . what should we do?"

"I'll ride Jim to see what it is. If it should be a grass fire, I'll come right back to plow a fire break, but if I see that it's in Bowbells, I'll go on to see what I can do."

"Oh. John, be careful."

"I will." And he galloped away.

Bowbells was a good six miles from the homestead, and he knew if it was in town that there would be little he could do once he'd get there, but he had to try. The notion that it could be a prairie grass fire was soon dispelled, and he rode on.

Still a half mile or so away, he could see the smoldering buildings sending plumes of smoke in to the air. There were men with black-streaked faces holding a shovel or a water bucket, standing about in disbelief and small clusters of crying women comforting one another.

Mr. Blenkner, owner of the mercantile, acknowledged John as he rode in with an uplifted hand, but when John asked in broken English if he could do anything to help, the man just shook his head.

It was a man named Savage who walked toward John. "You one of the homesteaders?"

John had dismounted and extended his hand. "Ja, I am John Adamson."

"We'll build again, and if you want to help, we'd be much obliged. We'll need to have building materials sent from somewhere, probably Minneapolis. Be a week or more, I expect, but we need to get it done before winter gets a hold. Need the general store and the bank at least. The post office was spared and the claims office and most of the homes. I don't think anyone was seriously injured, so we can rebuild."

John nodded his head and looking about at the smoldering ruins, he said, "Ja, I will help, and I will tell others." Mounting his horse, he rode toward home.

Mary and the children greeted him as he rode up and wanted to know what had happened.

As he dismounted, he said, "There was a bad fire in town. Most of the businesses are gone, but no one was hurt badly." Before he could say more, Mary Inga pouted. "What about the October Fest?"

"Nei, Mary," said her mother. "Don't talk so. The people in town are suffering, and you pout about a celebration? I am sure no one feels like celebrating."

"But Mor . . ."

"That's enough," John scolded, but Mary Inga began to cry. And raising her skirt, she ran toward the back of the shack.

"Mary Inga, come back here," shouted her father as he began to pursue her until Mary grabbed his arm.

"John, Mary is a young woman now. She will be fifteen years old in January and thinking of things not found on this homestead. She is disappointed because she's been looking forward to the October Fest ever since the festivities on the Fourth of July."

"Ja, I know, I know, but I keep thinking of the fire. All those buildings burned to the ground and the looks on the people's faces. But I will help to rebuild. It is our town too."

"When will you start?"

"As soon as the lumber comes from Minneapolis, in a week or two. I will ride to town in a week and see." And John led Jim to the corral.

Mary found Mary Inga seated on the bank of the creek just where she thought she would be. More and more often, she would disappear when her work was done or when she'd coaxed Emile and Dora into doing her work for her.

"Mary, you shouldn't have acted that way to your far."

"I know . . . I'm sorry, but I was so looking forward to going to town for the October Fest. Is Pa real mad at me?"

Mary sat down beside her daughter and said, "Nei, but you must apologize."

"Ja, I know."

"I will ask your far if we might have a few neighbors over before it gets too cold to be out of doors. We are having what they call an Indian summer, and perhaps it will last for a time."

"Oh, Mor, that would be wonderful." And then Mary dropped her eyes and said, "Do you think we could invite the Carlson family?"

"The Carlsons? Do we know them?" Mary teased. She knew that Mary Inga had spent quite a bit of time talking with the Carlson's son, Charlie, on the Fourth of July.

"Mor, you're teasing! You know we do."

They rose and started back to the shack, and Mary said, "I'll ask your Far tonight."

The day before everyone would arrive, Mary and Mary Inga were busy baking. It took so long in the small stovepipe oven, but they managed. By evening, there was an assortment of Danish pastries and two loaves of white bread, one of rye, and one of dark molasses bread.

Mary had had to limit the number of families she could ask, and she hoped the Hansons and Larsons would not be offended. They would have them alone at another time.

Jebbe, Thea, and the children were the first to arrive. Thea set a pork roast, covered to keep it from the ever-present flies on the table set up in the yard, and asked Mary what she could do to help.

"I think we are all ready, and as soon as the others come, we'll eat." Mary had no sooner said it than the Carlson team and wagon pulled into the yard. Mary and John didn't know them well since they lived some distance southwest and had never had any occasion the see them except when they met at the Fourth of July picnic in Bowbells. They were a large family with five boys, ranging in age from two to eighteen, with Charlie being the oldest. Mrs. Carlson was short and round while her husband, Charles, was tall and lanky, and the boys ranged in between.

After the introductions, they saw Andrew coming across the field, and the introductions started all over again once he was there.

Mrs. Carlson had brought a thick venison stew, so with the open-faced Danish sandwiches that Mary Inga had made, the pork roast from Thea, a plate of thick-sliced bread and one of Danish pastries, they all sat down to eat.

After dinner, the men went off in one direction while the women cleared the table and washed the dishes before sitting down to visit.

Mary Inga soon disappeared, and Mary saw that she was seated on the back of the Carlson wagon with Charlie at her side.

John and the other men were discussing the fire in Bowbells, and both John and Andrew had agreed to help with the rebuilding once the materials arrived.

"It's the very least we can do," John spoke out. "There isn't much time before winter, and we need a store and bank as much as anyone."

Andrew agreed, but Jebbe said, "Not me. I've got work of my own to do. Besides, those bigwigs have the money to hire it done."

"I agree! I've got plenty to do on my own place than to go into town to help them," said Carlson. "Are they going to pay you, Adamson?"

John was a little hot under the collar when he answered. "Nei, I don't need wages to help someone needing help. Those folks need help, and besides, just what would you do without a store to buy supplies? Have you thought of that?"

That was the end of the conversation about helping the folks in town, except when Andrew told John that he'd ridden in to see when they could get started. "A man by the name of Christianson told me everything will be there the first of the week, and he said they were going to build a school if there was time. I asked him about a school out our way, and he said there had been some talk of it. He said something about a man named Hansen starting one."

John said, "Come on by, and I'll ride along with you."

After everyone was gone, John said, "I hope Carlson's son isn't as ornery as his father." And he looked at Mary Inga who said, "I don't think he is." And she grinned.

Andrew came by on Tuesday, and the two of them rode into Bowbells.

They were prepared to stay over if they needed to and hoped that someone would feed them.

Several men were unloading a railroad car of lumber, and John and Andrew pitched in to help load it into wagons to be taken to the individual sights. Andrew asked where their help was most needed, and they were told that the general store and bank were to be built first, and they could work on whichever one they wanted. They chose the general store.

By noon, the posts were set for the foundation, and the sills and joists were in place and ready for the subfloor. There was no danger of going hungry because exactly at twelve o'clock, the men were all told to wash up and take a seat at the table set up for them. The women of the town had made sure that not a man would go hungry.

The end of the first day saw the subfloor on and the building framed. Clarence Pederson, one of the men they'd worked with, asked John, "Can you guys stay over, or do you have to go home?"

"Nei, we can stay. We'll bunk under a wagon and be up and ready in the morning."

"You'll do no such a thing. My missus said you're to come home with me. We got room."

"That's good of you, but there is no need—"

Pederson cut him off. "If I don't bring you home, my missus will skin me alive, and that's the truth."

Andrew answered for them both. "Well, if you put it that way, we'll come."

The next day saw more progress, and by the afternoon of the third day, the roof was sheeted and roofed. Only the windows and siding were left, and then they could start on the inside with wainscoting.

He'd been gone from home for three days and knew there were things to be done there, especially with winter coming on, but John decided to stay and help the others finish the job. Another day should do it, and Andrew agreed.

The stock for the store stood waiting in the immigrant shack until the inside of the store was finished and the shelves built. Everyone in town was anxious for the store to open, and a number of homesteaders had come into town to see the progress and stayed to lend a hand for a few hours or a day or so.

John wished he had the buckboard and team so he could buy what winter supplies they would need before he left for home, but it was only wishful thinking so he said, "I'll be back in a week or so for supplies." And they rode for home.

* * *

A school was built two sections west of the Adamson homestead, and Mary Inga, Pete, and Emil started school. Mary Inga and Pete had attended school in Denmark, and for two years in Iowa. But for Emil, it was the first time, and he wasn't sure whether or not he should go; but the day came, and he climbed aboard the buckboard with his sister and brother. Dora stood on the ground with tear streaks on her cheeks and waved as the wagon left the yard.

The following spring saw Mary Inga almost sixteen, with Charlie Carlson as a frequent guest. He had built a Soddy on the Carlson homestead, and the day after Mary's sixteenth birthday, on April 11, 1901, Mary Inga and Charlie Carlson were married.

A late snow that year brought a bumper crop to many, but John had planted wheat to his first eighty acres, a mistake because the ground was not ready in nutrients. He should have planted flax and wheat the next year. As a consequence, the yield was poor, with just enough grain for flour to see them through, and seed for the coming year and barely enough for feed for the animals. He had hoped to sell enough to buy some new implements and coal for the winter.

The sow had surprised them with fourteen little piglets early in the spring so come the Fourth of July, twelve of them accompanied the family to that year's Independence Day celebration, and by the afternoon, all twelve little pigs were sold as well as the young steer from the year before.

Before going home, John walked into the general store and ordered a cook stove with an oven from Ben Blenkner. He would have liked one with a water reservoir at the side, but since space was so limited, he bought the smallest one made and asked, "When will it come?"

"It'll come in from Minneapolis in about two weeks if they have one in stock. It's a shame you can't get one with a reservoir. I know the missus would like that."

"Just not enough room, Ben" was John's reply.

Mary sold cheese and garden vegetables that fall to buy enough yard goods for a dress for Dora and shirts for John and the boys, but Dora, Emil, and Pete would need new shoes before the winter.

Dora was put in charge of Ella whenever their mother was in the field or too busy to keep track of her. Ella was nearly always good natured, but when she was outside, she was hard to keep track of, wandering off toward the wheat fields or through the garden. Once when Mary was drawing water from the well, Ella had wandered into the field where the grain was taller than she was and it took some time to find her.

Mary was called on frequently to deliver a baby, often not knowing the family or their circumstances or needs, so she would take her basket of supplies, including food and extra bedding.

One such delivery had taught her to be prepared.

It was in the middle of the night as the family slept that someone pounded on the door, jarring John awake, and when he got up and opened the door, a man almost fell inside. He was dirty and disheveled and spoke in broken German. "You got to come, it's my missus."

By this time, Mary was up and getting herself dressed. While she gathered the things she usually took along, John had fed the fire and pulled the coffee pot over the flame to heat quickly and sliced some bread and pushed it before the man. Mary looked at the man who seemed to be little more than a sack of bones and added a loaf of bread and a generous wedge of cheese and tucked some cookies around the edge. The man was in a hurry, but when he saw the bread John had moved to the edge of the table, he looked at John for permission and snatched a piece, and without butter or cheese, devoured the whole piece in two bites and took another with him as they went out the door.

Once at the man's home, Mary was sickened by the squalor. Four small children as scrawny as their father stood huddled in a corner while their mother labored on a straw tick in the opposite corner. The stove had gone out, and it was cold. The man obviously cared about his family, but the North Dakota Prairie and a sickly wife must have defeated him.

After examining the frail little woman, it was clear the baby had to be turned in the womb, and the woman was so weak that Mary wondered at the outcome. But at last, a small baby boy was born, and the woman seemed to rally. Mary, in the meantime, had instructed her husband to take a note to John, asking him to give the man some fuel for his fire and more food and then added bedding and Ella's outgrown baby things. She and John had little to spare themselves, but here, the need was greater.

* * *

Mrs. Ole Olson was a stern, unsmiling woman but not without a certain sense of humor.

Mary had seen little of her since that first Fourth of July picnic when she'd corrected Thea and herself about their language. But one day, Mrs. Olson came in a buggy behind her white mare and stopped in the yard. She had come, she said, "to acquaint herself with the making of cheese." As she put it, "in exchange for English-speaking instructions."

Mary didn't know whether to be offended or pleased at first until Mrs. Olson said, "More is the pity that I have nothing more to offer."

"You needn't offer me anything to know how I make my cheese, but I would be ever grateful to learn better English. Of course, I have learned some from living in America as long as we have, but I would like to speak without stumbling over the words. John has learned more American, or I should say English, but we use German most of the time because it is easier."

"You are Danes, are you not?"

Mary nodded. "Ja, we are, but our part of Denmark is occupied by Germany, and we were not allowed to speak anything but German."

With that, Mrs. Olson stiffened, and looking quite righteous, said, "Well, all right then, when should we begin?"

"Now would be good."

"Now? Well, all right then." And she climbed down from the buggy and led the mare to a post and tied her there before following Mary into the shack. With a cup of coffee and a plate of molasses bread and cheese before her, she began to point to different objects about the room. The first item was the cheese. "Cheese."

And Mary repeated, "Cheese." It soon became clear that Mary knew more English than she had thought, but now it was to put it together in sentences.

The afternoon passed quickly, but when she left, Mrs. Olson held a wedge of cheese and a form for molding her first attempt at making cheese in her lap as she started off for home.

When John came in from the field, Mary greeted him in English. "Hello, John. How are you today?"

John grinned and said, also in English, "I am well, Mary. What will we have for supper?" and from then on, a greater effort was made to speak the language of their new country.

The homestead was proved up enough to warrant the deed of ownership by the fall of 1902, but the other eighty acres had scarcely seen the plow. The year 1902 saw the Adamson's first grandchild too when Mary Inga delivered her first baby, a little girl they named Grace, the first of Mary Inga and Charlie Carlson's family. Later, there would be Carl, Wallace, and Viola.

In 1904, the crops were good, and things were looking up, so John bought another team of horses and some new machinery. The barn was made bigger, and by adding another small room, it enlarged the homestead shack, but it was still small.

School was in session most of the late fall and winter, and John took Emil, who everyone by now was calling Mill, and Dora in the sled behind Jim, when the weather was too bad to walk.

There was a French family with boys, Francis and Louie, and a girl named Dullis who homesteaded just west of the school. When the weather was clear enough to walk, Dora and Dullis would walk together as far as their Soddy, and Mill would walk with the boys. The boys would set snares on the way to school, and if they were lucky, they'd have snared some gophers, which they'd skin and hang on a tripod over a fire to roast on the way home. It sounded awful, but since Mill seemed to like them, Dora decided to try one; and to her surprise, she liked them too. "Tastes like quail, don't you think?" she asked, but Dullis wrinkled her nose. "I've tasted them," and she wrinkled her nose again.

Mill and Dora spoke very good English by now and no longer lapsed into German. Not even when their folks did, though they could understand what was being said. So when Mary told Dora that Mrs. Olson wanted her to work for her two weeks in the summer and two weeks in the spring, Dora felt privileged. She knew what importance Mrs. Olson put on speaking the English language instead of any foreign tongue. She would say, "In America, be an American!" And she made no bones about it, regardless of who was around.

Dora had turned ten years old in February, and she was to start working for Mrs. Olson the first week of nice weather, and so she did. Mrs. Olson had set up two washtubs on a bench in the yard and helped Dora fill one with hot water and the other lukewarm. Beside the washstand were two large cloth bags full of dirty clothes to be washed, a scrub board, and a bar of strong lye soap.

Dora knew how to wash clothes, she'd helped her mother many times, and so she began. A shirt of Mr. Olson was dirty but not bad, a baby's romper, a bib, one of Mrs. Olson's dresses but then. "What was that?" It felt like a hard lump of something, and that it was a diaper that hadn't been rinsed out or even emptied. "Offda!" was all she could say. She'd seen a kitchen knife lying on the bench but had paid it no mind until now. Now she knew its intent and scraped the diaper before putting it in a pail of water left standing at the side of the bench to soak before it was washed. That diaper was one of many.

Dora was never so glad to see the end of those two weeks of Mrs. Olson's chores so she could be home to help her mother. Her small hands were red and sore from the strong lye soap, and when Mary saw them, she said. "Oh my, what did Mrs. Olson have you do?"

"Lots of stuff, but mostly washing clothes." And she told her mother about the bags of dirty clothes and about the diapers.

At the thought of prim Mrs. Olson letting her wash go that long and the dirty diapers, "Oh my!" and Mary could not help but smile until she saw tears gathering in Dora's eyes.

"Oh, den lille. I am not smiling about how hard you worked. Nie, it is about Mrs. Olson." And she explained how the thought of the prim, snobbish woman and her dirty clothes made her smile.

It had been a very long time since Mary had taken her journal from the trunk to write anything, and one afternoon, she sat down in the shade of the house. And thinking back to where she'd left off she began to write:

> So many things have happened. Mary Inga was married in 1901 just after her sixteenth birthday, and now we have two grandchildren, Grace and Carl, and soon there will be another.
>
> Pete is almost a man and works for other farmers when he isn't helping John. Emil, who we call Mill, works with John and goes to school. He is a fine boy and sometimes I think John is too hard on him. I wish John could leave his own terrible childhood behind, but it is so much a part of him that I fear he never will. It is difficult to understand why he is so hard on his family when he himself had it so hard, but I suppose I will never understand, and John has a wonderful and kind side as well like how gentle he is with the animals or if any of us are sick.
>
> Dora is ten now and has started to work for Mrs. Olson once in a while to earn some money. She is saving it for something, but I don't know what. She doesn't like to wash clothes for Mrs. Olson.

Elsie, we call her Ella, is seven and is a big help to me, but she is the only one that John spoils, but she is a good girl even so.

We have had good crops and bad, but all in all this North Dakota Prairie has been good but hard.

Per and Marie and the children came from Iowa and rented a farm west of here. It was so good to see them and especially Marie, but once they were settled, we saw little of them. The winter that year was so bad, and then before we knew it, Per decided to move to Canada. We talk of going to see them, and I hope we can one day.

I think of the captain in Denmark each time I write in my journal since it was he who gave it to me when we came to America, now so long ago it seems, and I still wonder about Dora who cooked for him and after whom our little Dora Amelia Tora was named.

Mary returned the journal to the trunk and started supper with the thoughts of what she'd written twirling around in her mind. It was hot, and she would have liked to hitch up her long dress and let the breeze cool her legs, but there was no time for such nonsense, so she tucked the little damp curls from around her face back in place and hurried to the root cellar.

* * *

A dark-haired, wiry young man stepped from the train when it lumbered to a stop at the Bowbells station. Throwing his coat over one shoulder and hanging a canvas satchel of carpenter tools over the other, he picked up his valise and stood for a moment, looking up and down the stations platform, trying to decide which way to go. He'd come looking for work after hearing of a fire that had burned much of the town and that they were hiring carpenters to rebuild. He'd been the only passenger to get off the train and watched as two wagons went by toward the freight cars loaded with lumber at the end of the train and decided to see if he could be of any help.

Approaching the driver of the second wagon, he hollered up, "You want some help?" He spoke in a heavy Norwegian accent, and the driver grinned down at him and said, "Ya, *by yiminy*." Sam set his belongings on the platform and reached up to shake hands, saying, "Sam Berg!" As they exchanged names, "Ole Knutson." And a friendship that would last for years to come began.

Sam had emigrated from Norway via Liverpool, England, in 1904 and worked in Minnesota and then in Minot, North Dakota. An older brother, Osten, Ed as he was called, had immigrated to America in 1888 and was a photographer in Minnesota and another brother, Anton, came in 1892 and lived in Minnesota as well. A third brother, Ole, came in 1902 to Minnesota and then to Minot. It was a practice then that the first of a family to emigrate, once he was established, would send for the next who wanted to come and so on. And so it was how Sam had come.

Sam asked about a place to stay once the wagon was loaded and was directed to the hotel that had miraculously escaped the fire. It was the second fire to have devastated the town in just a few years.

At the hotel, he took a room and had his dinner in the dining room before finding the man doing the hiring. He was put to work the next morning on the Megg building, but when his finishing skills were noted, he was sent to work on the Bowbells school house and from there to another and another job. He was a good carpenter and soon came into demand. He was asked to build a house for Charlie and Mary Inga Carlson, and when it was finished, they told him about Mary Inga's father and mother, the Adamsons, who wanted an addition built to their house. It was some time before he could get out to the Adamson place to inquire about the job, having an addition to finish on the bank in town, and it was taking more time than he'd planned.

It started to rain and didn't let up for days. The downpour made the streets a sea of mud ankle deep, and one day as he was driving his horse and buggy down the street in front of the general store, a girl came from the store and stood on the wooden walkway just as he passed, sending mud flying up to spatter her dress, and she hollered at him angrily.

"Oh, you olf! Look what you've done to my dress."

Sam pulled up to apologize, but when he saw how angry the girl was, he couldn't help but grin as he said, "I am very sorry."

"You do not look very sorry to me! Just look at my dress!"

Sam had become sober and apologized again. "I really am sorry. Can I buy you a new dress?"

The girl said, "No, thank you!" And she turned and huffed away.

Sam felt bad about the incident, and yet he still could not help but chuckle at the girl's reaction.

By the time the bank building was finished, the rain had stopped, so early the following morning, Sam put his tools in the buggy and started for the Adamson farm.

It was going to be a hot day, but a soft breeze stirred the blue flowering flax, causing the fields of blue to shimmer in the early morning sun. The countryside was like a patchwork quilt of blue flax and golden wheat, and Sam let the horse go at its own easy lope while he sat back enjoying the morning when a picture of his mother in Norway came to mind and brought sudden tears to his eyes. If only she could be here, he thought, *She would love it so*. So different from the rocky soil they'd tried to farm in Norway. But his father, he knew would never leave the homeland.

As he thought about his mother, the mountains where he'd spent many hours with the horses on the Satre came to mind, and he had to smile. And then he thought about his good friend, Krist Trastad, who had spent some of those times on the Satre with him as they herded horses, and he thought of a time the two of them had taken a fancy to two milkmaids at a nearby farm, and they'd asked him and Krist to take supper with them.

One of the girls said, "We have permission from the cook to ask you. We'll be having our supper in the kitchen." But when the time came, the owner of the farm came to the kitchen, and seeing two strange boys, she said, "What is the meaning of this?" And the cook had gone back on them and chased them from her kitchen so not to get herself in trouble.

He and Krist had left in a hurry with an empty stomach, and once they got back to the pasture where the horses were supposed to be, the horses were nowhere in sight. One of the horses was a stallion and had been giving them some trouble by wanting to go back down the mountain, but they thought he had given up on the idea by then, and they felt safe in leaving them for the time it would take to eat a super they'd been invited to. They were wrong, and it took until the next morning to find them.

The path the horses took was clear, and they found them standing at the gate of their home paddock. He and Krist had tried in vain to herd them back up the mountain to the satre when the horse's owner came to help, after blaming the horses for the whole thing, and Sam and Krist didn't tell him otherwise.

Sam thought of his mother again. Had she known what he and Krist had done, he would have felt the wrath of his father.

Again, Sam smiled to himself and continued to daydream. This time, about the big flat rock where the mice played, he thought about how he'd made the tiny harnesses out of coarse threads he pulled from his pants, and how he'd played with them. He could still remember how the mice pulled a small tree branch behind them before he let them go.

Sam was determined to be as American as he could be, though he couldn't rid himself of a strong Norwegian accent, nor could he adapt his skills completely to the system of measurement used in America. Though he was getting better at it, he nearly always reverted back to the metric system he was so familiar with.

Krist Trastad, he wondered what had become of him. He'd accompanied him to America and to Minnesota, but Krist had chosen to stay in Minnesota when Sam and his brother Ole went to find work in Minot. As he thought of Krist, he said to himself, "I'll look him up as soon as I can."

The Adamson farm came into view, and Sam clucked his tongue for the horses to move along.

Turning in, he stopped near the house and tied the reins to the brake and stepped down, but as he did, he spotted a girl coming from the chicken coop with a basket of eggs. He recognized her immediately as the girl he'd splashed mud on in Bowbells. Mumbling under his breath, he said, "Oh no. I hope she doesn't remember me."

But remember him she did and stopped short a few feet from him. "You. What is it you want?"

"I've come to see John Adamson. Is he your father?"

"Ja, he is," but before she could say any more, John came from the barn to greet the stranger.

"I am John Adamson." And he held out his hand to the younger man. "But I know you. You built my daughter and son-in-law's house. What is your name again?"

"Sam Berg! Charlie said you want some building done."

"Ja, I do. Come and I'll show you."

Just then, Mary came from the house to see who was there, and John said, "Sam, this is my wife, Mary." And Sam took her hand in greeting.

Mary looked at Dora and asked Sam, "Did you meet our daughter, Dora?"

Sam could feel his face turn red as he tipped his hat in Dora's direction and said, "Dora."

And Dora responded with, "Sam." But at this point, it was hard for either to keep a straight face, and Dora looked at her mother and said, "Ma, this is the man who splashed mud all over me."

Mary smiled, "Oh I see," and no more was said about it.

The two men walked about, deciding on the new structure to be built, and with that in mind, they planned for the sort of building materials to use.

"I can draw up a blueprint," Sam offered. "So we'll know how much lumber to order. If that's all right? I can have the blueprint done in a couple of days and bring it out for you to see. Then you can order your lumber."

"Ja! That would be good. Now we will have coffee." And they went inside where Mary set a cup of coffee and a plate of fresh molasses bread and cheese before them on the table. Dora studied the man sitting next to her father from the open doorway until her mother asked.

"Dora, did you want something to eat?"

Flustered, she said, "Oh no, thank you, Ma." And she turned and fled to the barn.

As promised, Sam brought the blueprints he'd drawn to the Adamsons' a few days later with a list of materials he would need to begin building. After examining the blueprints, John asked, "When you get back to town, will you order the material for me? I believe this will cover the cost," and he handed Sam some money.

Sam was asked to stay for supper, and seated around the table, he was asked about his family and homeland. He told them about his brothers who were already in America and about the brothers and sisters still in Norway. "My sister, Anna, is married, and she will come to join her husband, Fritjof, in Montana soon. They have four children—Marit, Astrid, Finn, and Magnhild. I hope I can see them when they come."

"Will all of your family come here?" Mary asked.

"I don't know, but I know my mother and father will not come. I will go home one day to see them."

"Ja, that will be good," Mary said. "I hope to go back to see my brothers and sisters one day as well."

John scowled, "I have no one there to see."

"You have my family and the captain and Bjorn," Mary reminded.

"Ja, I know."

Then he said, "I have a brother. He came to North Dakota, but I guess he didn't like it because he moved his family to Canada. He is a bit of an adventurer."

When the building material came, John and Jebbe took their wagons to town to unload it from the train.

Sam worked long hours to get the house closed in and ready for the plaster before the first snow fell, and the family could hardly wait for it to be finished. What had been the tarpaper shack was now the kitchen, and a living room and dinning room were added to it with three bedrooms upstairs. It was indeed a wonderful thing to have so much room, and a week before Christmas they were moved in.

One evening, Mary asked John if they could ask Sam to stay for Christmas. They had become very fond of him, and it seemed only fitting since he had no family near.

"Ja, that would be good." And so it was that Christmas Eve Sam stood with his hat lying on top of a box that he carried when the door was opened.

"Come in, Sam, come in." John stood back to let him pass.

Sam carried the box to the table, and Mary said, "Oh my. Mange takk, but you did not have to bring anything."

Ella was excited. "Open it, Ma!"

Mary looked at Sam as if asking his permission, and he said, "Ja, open it. Maybe you will want to use it."

She unwrapped a dinner plate with small pink flowers around the edge and a cup of the same pattern. She hardly knew what to say as tears ran down her cheeks. "They are so beautiful. You shouldn't have."

"Nei, it is nothing. It is for your new house and to say mange takk for all the good suppers you have given me and for asking me to share the Christmas Yule with your family."

Dora and Ella set the table with the new dishes while John and Sam went to the barn to give the animals and birds their traditional Christmas feeding.

* * *

In the spring, Sam built a new barn and silo for the Adamsons who were prospering after having some good crops and an increase in good cattle and prices were up to a dollar for young hogs. The slim years seemed to be behind them.

Jebbe and Thea came one day in the early fall to ask about butchering since the two families always did this together.

When Thea stepped down from the buggy, Mary could see that something was wrong.

"Thea, you are so pale, is something wrong?"

"I have not been feeling well, but it will pass."

"You need not help in the butchering, Thea, I and Dora can manage. And Mary Inga can come to help."

"Nei, I'll come. It will probably do me good." And Mary knew it was no use to argue with her sister.

But the day came to butcher, and Thea did not come to help. Jebbe excused her by saying, "Ja, she is a bit under the weather."

"Has she been to the doctor?"

Jebbe stiffened at the idea. "Nei, she'll be back on her feet in no time. Doesn't need a doctor to tell her that she's a bit on the lazy side."

Mary bristled and was about to attack Jebbe with what she thought of his innuendo about his wife when John put his hand firmly on Mary's arm and said calmly, "It wouldn't hurt to see the doctor, Jebbe. Maybe he could give her a tonic to give her more energy."

"Say, that might be a good idea." And the subject was changed.

When the meat was attended to and the sausage made, Mary went to visit her sister.

"Thea, you need to see the doctor. Do you want me to take you?"

"Nei, Jebbe will take me tomorrow. He thinks the doctor will give me some tonic. I'm sure it's all I need."

"Ja, well, I'm glad you are going. Let me know what he says."

And then Thea asked, "Have you heard from home lately? It seems like a long time since anyone has written."

"No, I haven't," said Mary. "I'd have told you if I had, but I haven't written for some time myself."

Jebbe and Thea stopped on their way home from Bowbells, and sitting at the table with a cup of coffee, Thea told Mary what the doctor had said. "He gave me tonic just as Jebbe said he would. He said I am anemic. I told him that I had suffered with that as a child, and he was not surprised. Remember Mary when I was to eat all that liver? I dislike liver to this day." Then she took a letter from her pocket. "A letter from home. Will you read it aloud?" And she handed it to Mary who opened it and began to read.

> My dear sisters and all,
>
> It is such a long time since we have heard from you. We pray that you are all well and prospering.
>
> We in the family are well, but not without worry for our brothers. Frederick has been transferred to Hamburg so we do not see him. He was to see Elsie and the children once, but only for a few hours.
>
> Heinrick is still near, so we see him on occasion, but he is always in that dreadful German uniform. Helga comes to see us with the children whenever she can. She tells us that Heinrick too will be transferred soon, probably nearer to Berlin. She and the children will move to wherever he goes if they are allowed to, but of course,

since she is German, it might make a difference. I hope so for Heinrick's sake. But we are ever grateful that neither has been in battle.

Now I must tell you the sad news that your youngest brother, our own dear Christian, has been taken into the German Army as well. I do not know where he will be sent, but be assured that he is in good spirits as he always is.

You asked if there is a way for you to write to your brothers, but at present, I do not know.

Lana and her family are well, and she sends her love. Her husband is a watchmaker.

I seldom see Anna, but whenever I do, she is expecting a baby. The last time I saw her, she said she was going to write to you, and I hope she has.

I am aging and my hair has turned white, but I am well.

You asked again about the captain and about his cook, Dora, in particular. I am sad to say that it has been a long while since I saw the captain, and then when I mentioned his cook, he avoided my question. I have to say that I too am curious. Perhaps I will ask Frederick's Elsie to go to visit the captain and inquire about his cook, Dora. Elsie is so good to talk to people and everyone likes her.

I have nothing more to tell you about Dorthea except that I do see her on occasion, but as always, either at a distance or when she is rushed away, but she always smiles. Have you corresponded with her since I sent you the address?

I will close for now, and I look forward to hearing from you soon.

Your tanta, Dorthea

As Mary folded the letter and put it back inside the envelope, her eyes filled with tears as she looked at Thea who was wiping her tears away with the back of her hand. Neither one said a word for a moment until Thea burst out, "Oh, Mary, our poor Christian."

"Ja, our dear Christian," said Mary. "I was so hoping he would not have to go, but I know it was only wishful thinking. I wish we could write to him, to all three of them."

"Ah, Mary, I do too."

Mary wondered if her sister had written to her Dorthea, but she didn't want to ask for fear of upsetting her, but she didn't have to because Thea answered the unspoken question.

"Tanta Dorthea asked if I had written to my Dorthea, and I am ashamed to say that I have not. I just cannot make myself do it. What is wrong with me that I cannot write to my own daughter?"

"You are simply afraid to open up old wounds, Thea. The baby you hold in your heart is now a young woman, but a young woman who needs to know her mother. A young woman who is now old enough to understand the circumstances under which you both exist."

"I know you are right, Mary, and I will write to her. I will, I must. But all I can see is that baby who was snatched from my arms."

Mary was grateful that John and Jebbe came in just then to ward away the emotional outbursts that ensued each time Thea talked of her Dorthea.

"Is the coffee hot?" John asked as they sat down.

"Ja, and cream cake too."

It was not long after this that Thea's health began to deteriorate, and Jebbe decided to sell the homestead and move into town. When Sam Berg heard of it, he offered to buy the farm and much of Jebbe's machinery, and a deal was struck. To think, he had a farm of his own, and it was so near the Adamsons. It was just what he'd been dreaming of. But since he had unfinished work in Bowbells, he would remain there until spring, or so he thought, until an unpredicted burst of springlike weather beckoned him into the field, and he found himself dividing his time between the two.

Farming in North Dakota was far different than in Norway. There they had farmed in light, rocky soil, and here it was mostly heavy gumbo. The implements and machinery too were different, and even the way in which it was done. No one dried hay here by hanging it over a fence.

The Ole Hansons had built a barn that summer and decided to have a barn dance since summer seemed to have returned in October. Mary, Dora, and Mary Inga helped by preparing food, and Andrew Peterson promised to play his harmonica, and Sven Larson would play the accordion.

It was a warm Friday evening, and everyone came dressed in their best. Dora was especially excited because that summer, a boy by the name of Harry White, whose father owned the threshing outfit, came to their farm to help thresh their grain. And he'd smiled and winked at her when she and her mother served the men their dinner. He went to school in Bowbells, and Dora had only seen him at a few doings in town before that, but he might be at the dance.

Many of the homesteaders and a few people from town were there when the music started, and Harry was the first to ask Dora to dance. They were playing a square dance, and H. C. was calling, "Take your partner and doe-se-doe, around the ring and there you go . . ."

John and Mary hadn't danced in such a long time. They waited for a slow one to begin and when Sven and Andrew struck up "Coming through the Rye," John took Mary's hand and led her to the dance floor, and before long, they were dancing to whatever was being played.

Sam Berg and Ole Knutson came in just as lunch was being served and found a place by the wall to stand until John motioned for them to help themselves to the food.

When the music started up again, Sam made his way to a bench where Dora Adamson sat next to Harry White. Dora and Harry were just getting up to go on the dance floor when Sam reached for Dora's hand and said, "Can I have this dance?"

Dora rolled her eyes and said, "Oh, all right." And she excused herself from Harry.

They were playing a schottische, and Dora found herself being whirled and dipped as Sam spun her around and caught her as he led her into the next step.

When the music stopped, Dora couldn't say a word. She just looked at him.

Sam, still holding Dora's hand, led her toward the musicians and asked if they could play the Swedish Waltz, and as they started to play, he led her to the floor and the dance began. Dora had never danced the Swedish Waltz before, but she soon caught on, and they whirled about the floor.

Harry cut in on the next dance, and Dora went back and forth between the two for the rest of the evening until her mother handed her her wrap and said it was time to go home.

That night, as John and Mary lay in bed, Mary said, "Sam is quite the dancer, isn't he?"

"Ja, but Harry White is more Dora's age. I think Sam is twenty-seven, and Dora is but fifteen."

"John! I wasn't talking about marriage, I was talking about dancing."

"Ja, I know, but don't you think Sam is too old for her?"

"John!"

Sam was a frequent visitor to the Adamsons, and it soon became apparent that he and Dora were smitten with each other. Sam always offering to help Dora with her outside chores—milking or gathering eggs or they'd walk along Stony Creek in search of some obscure thing or reason, and then one day, Sam approached John. "I know that I am a lot older than Dora, twelve years as a matter of fact, but I love your daughter."

"Have you told her so?"

"Ja, I have, and she loves me too."

"So, what is it you are saying?"

"With your permission, I would like to marry Dora."

"Sam, Dora is not yet sixteen."

"Ja, I know, and I know we must wait until she is."

"I will have to talk to Dora's mor before I can give you an answer."

"Ja, sure!"

It was soon after that when the matter was discussed again, and then it was Dora who did the asking.

"Ma, has Pa talked to you about Sam and me getting married?"

"Ja, he has, but Dora, Sam is so much older than you. It is not that we don't like him, we do, very much but . . ."

"Oh, Ma, please. I really love him."

"I will talk to your far again, and we will see."

"Thank you, Ma."

The weather had turned bitterly cold, freezing even the water in the well and making it necessary to send Mil, with one foot in the bucket, down to crack a hole in the ice. But as his full weight went to the bucket, the rope snapped and he plummeted, bucket and all to the frozen surface of the well; and breaking a hole in the ice, he fell beneath the ice and into the freezing water. In a moment, John was reaching with one hand for Mil, but it was too far. Mil's head was now above the water, and John yelled, "Hold on! I'll get a rope." He raced toward the barn. He was back in minutes and soon had his son out of the well, his foot still wedged inside the bucket and shaking with the wet and cold.

Once Mil was inside and changed into dry, warm clothes, he grinned at John. "There's a big hole in the ice now, Pa."

Mary, who was pouring coffee, said, "Ja, and you could have been drowned."

Soon after that, Sam borrowed Andrew's sleigh and came to the Adamsons in hopes of taking Dora on a sleigh ride, and with the hope that John would give them his blessing to be married.

When the door was opened, he took off his hat and stepped inside, but before he could say a word, Mary had him led to the table. "Sit down, Sam, you must be half frozen." And he was handed a cup of coffee and a plate of bread and cheese was set before him.

"Nei! It has warmed up some." Taking a sip of coffee, he said, "Mange takk."

"Here, have something to eat," as she pushed the plate closer to him.

As he spread butter on a slice of bread and laid on a piece of cheese and folded it over, he said, "I was wondering if Dory could come for a sleigh ride. I borrowed Andrew's sleigh."

Just then, Dora came into the room. "Did you just call me Dory? You must have been listening to Mil. He's called me that since I was little." Then she turned to her mother. "Can I go for a sleigh ride? I'll dress warm!"

Mary smiled and patted her on the shoulder. "Ja, I suppose you have something to tell him. Come back before dark." And Sam assured her they would.

Once they were in the sleigh and starting off, Sam asked, "What do you have to tell me? Can you marry me?"

She shouted, "Yes! Yes I can . . . just as soon as I have my birthday." And she threw her arms about his neck.

Dora's birthday was February 7, and plans were laid for the wedding.

Sam was half expecting his brother Ole, who was also a carpenter, to come to work on a job in Bowbells, but he'd almost given up on him when one day as he was loading his wagon to go out to the farm someone called, "Syver." Turning around, he saw Ole coming toward him. Ole still called him Syver, and of course, it was his real name, the name he'd been born with; but an Irishman in Minnesota had pinned him with the name of Sam, and it had stuck, and he liked it more than Syver. So for all intrinsic purposes, he was Sam.

"Ole, I almost gave up on you. I told Anderson you were coming. He wants a house built on his homestead."

"Ja, Ja, I meant to be here sooner, but I had another job at the last minute that paid good. Why didn't you build this Anderson's house? Are you getting lazy?" And they both laughed as Sam put an arm about Ole's shoulder. Ole was a little shorter and stockier than Sam, but anyone could tell they were brothers.

Filling Ole in on what he knew of their family, Sam said, "Anton and Annie and the boys are here. They bought out a homestead in Dimond Township, quite a-ways southwest of the Adamsons."

"Who are the Adamsons?"

"Oh, that's right, you don't know. I am being married to Dora Adamson in just a few weeks. Her folks have a homestead about six miles southeast of here." Sam continued, "Dora and I have been out to Anton's a time or two, and maybe you and I can go out there tomorrow. Hop up, and we'll go out to my place."

"That's right, you bought up a homestead too. But what is this job you were telling me about?"

"It will wait a day or two!"

The next morning, Sam and Ole made the trip out to Anton and Annie's, and on the way, Ole asked, "What are their boys' names? I've forgotten."

"Leonard and Clarence!"

"That's right. I've never seen them, but I met Annie once in Minnesota."

Anton was in the field when they got there, but as they looked out over their brother's land, they saw him coming with the team, and as he drew near, Sam realized the strong resemblance he had to their father in Norway. A much slighter build, but so like him otherwise, even in disposition.

When he saw them, he waved and walked toward them. "Well I'll be . . . if it isn't Ole. Where did you find him, Syver?"

The day passed quickly, and on the way back to Bowbells, Sam said, "I'm going by the Adamsons so you can meet Dora."

Dora came from the house as they pulled up and stood waiting as they got down. "Dory, this is my brother Ole. We just came from Anton and Annie's."

"Hello, I'm pleased to meet you."

And the two shook hands before Ole said, "By yiminy, Syver, you have found a fine girl."

Dora blushed and smiled at Ole but questioned Sam, "Syver?"

"You remember, I told you how I got the name of Sam . . ."

"Oh, Ja, I remember . . . from an Irishman in Minnesota."

* * *

The next weeks were busy as Sam worked to get as much done in the fields as he could, and with the wedding coming up, he wanted the house to look as good as it could for Dora.

The Skow house was square with a kitchen, dining room, front room, and one bedroom downstairs and three bedrooms up. He'd bought furniture from the Sears Roebuck catalog and Thea had left behind enough cooking utensils and dishes for Dora to begin housekeeping.

It was cold but sunny the day Sam took Dora to be his wife. They were married in the Adamsons' parlor with friends and relatives in attendance. Dora wore the dress her mother made for her of white organdy with ruffles over the shoulders and long sleeves. She was beautiful, especially to Sam. It was March 22, 1912.

Though they didn't face the same hardships as when Dora's parents came to homestead, their work was cut out for them, and they worked long days side by side to get a crop in and a garden planted. But there was always time to sit on the banks of Stony Creek to laugh and plan for the future.

It was soon obvious that Dora was with child when she had to run to the outhouse to throw up and was having dizzy spells. The same symptoms Mary Inga explained to her of when she was first expecting Grace. "You'll get over it, it only lasts a short while."

Sam, Ole, and Anton had sent the fare for their brother, Christ, and his bride, Olivia, to come to America, and they were to arrive in early August. Sam and Dora had invited them to stay with them until they could get settled, but soon after they arrived, Dora saw there was a problem. Olivia spoke and understood only Norwegian, and Dora spoke only English and understood but a few words of Norwegian. She understood some Danish and German from living at home with her parents, but she and Sam were of the same mind regarding American English. To be in America was to speak and live as an American. It was a matter of pride, though they would never turn their backs on their Scandinavian heritage. America was their home, and they were grateful for it.

One night, as they crawled into bed, Dora said, "I cannot stand this any longer. Olivia can't speak English, and I cannot speak Norwegian. If we are to be in the same house, I need to be able to speak to her, or at least be able to understand her. She puts no effort into learning English. Will you teach me some Norwegian?"

"Ya, sure!" And the lessons began and continued each night as they lay in bed. One night, they started to giggle and laughter ensued, concluding their night's lesson, and Sam said, "Here we are, trying to be good Americans, and I am teaching you Norwegian." And they burst out laughing again.

The next morning, Olivia was crosser than usual and looked at the two of them with reproach.

Dora whispered in Sam's ear, "Do you suppose she heard us?"

He grinned. "It seems so. I wonder if she understood what we said."

"She couldn't! She doesn't understand English." And they could barely keep from laughing out loud.

Later, Dora admonished their banter and said, "We shouldn't make fun of Olivia. She will learn in time. I think she is just stubborn. I wonder . . . maybe she really didn't want to come here. Maybe it was all Christ's idea, and if that's the case, we should feel sorry for her. Don't you think?"

"Ja, you are right." But Dora could see the merriment in his eyes.

It was about this time when Krist Trastad showed up in Bowbells and bought a homestead near Sam and Dora, and Dora soon heard of all the pranks Krist and Sam had played in Norway as boys. She learned too that Krist was a good neighbor and friend. He had never married though he was older than Sam.

They butchered the first of November, and though Dora was expecting their first child, she was busy scraping casings for sausage while her mother and Olivia cut the meat to put in the crocks. Sam had enlisted Krist Trastad to do the killing. He would do anything to keep from doing it himself.

A few days later, Dora went into labor and Sam went to get Dora's mother. When he came back with Mary, Olivia was rushing about giving orders to anyone and everyone. Christ had been ordered out to bring more wood for the fire, Sam was scolded for not being there, but when she pointed her finger at Mary, it was her undoing. For Mary quietly took Olivia by the arm and led her to the stairway and pointed her finger up the stairs, but Olivia continued to rant, "*Davlin!*" Until Mary said, "*Tidig.*" And Olivia flew up the stairs in a huff.

A few hours later, Margaret Olga was born and Sam and Dora's family had begun. It was November 5, 1912.

Christ and Olivia rented a farm in Clayton Township right after Margaret was born and soon started a family of their own, but one day, when Sam and Dora were in town, Dora and the baby went into what was then Simonson's Market and saw Olivia over in the corner talking to someone. Olivia's back was to her as she went to say hello, and when she got close, she heard Olivia speaking in quite good English. She tapped Olivia on the shoulder, and when she turned around, Dora said hello in deliberately spoken Norwegian, and Olivia stammered and got red in the face. The two never spoke of the incident or about those few months in the same house.

Ella came almost every day when she was through with her chores to help with Margaret so Dora could join Sam in the field, or do what she had to. But one day, Ella decided to surprise her sister and cook supper. There was a jar of canned beef in the cupboard and vegetables in the garden, so she was going to make a stew and dumplings. When she opened the jar that she thought was beef, she saw that it was minced fine, but thought it was probably meant to be that way. She emptied it into a kettle and added cut-up carrots, potatoes, cabbage, onion, and water, and put it on to cook. She knew you never tasted meat from a jar until it was cooked, or you could be getting ptomaine poisoning. When it came to a boil, Ella thought it had kind of a funny smell, but maybe Dora had added some sort of spice to the meat. It didn't smell bad, just peculiar. After a few minutes, she pulled it to the back of the stove to simmer slowly while she mixed the dumplings. Now, everything was ready except to add the dumplings to steam. She would do that when she saw Mary and Sam coming from the field. Margaret was beginning to fuss as she played on the floor, and Ella picked her up and changed her diaper and then sat down to rock her. Margaret stuck her thumb in her mouth and smiled around it when Ella tickled her tummy.

The next thing she knew was Sam and Dora stomping the dirt from their feet on the porch. *Oh well, the dumplings will only take a few minutes,* she thought and waited for them to come in, but when the door opened, Dora began to sniff. "What is that smell?"

"Stew!" Ella beamed. "I made supper."

"Stew? It smells like something else. What did you put in it?"

"A jar of canned meat and vegetables."

"Canned meat?"

"I found it up in the cupboard there." Ella pointed to where it had been.

Dora went to the pot and lifted the lid, and when she did, she saw the mistake and said, "Well I guess we'll be having mincemeat stew."

Ella's face had turned red as a beet, and she was about to cry when Dora pushed her shoulder playfully with her hand. "It's all right, maybe you have come up with a new recipe."

In the meantime, Sam had taken a spoon and lifted the lid, tasted the concoction, and said, "Um, not bad. Might need a little salt."

Dora smiled, "And a few dumplings." And she spooned the dumpling dough on top of the stew and put on the lid.

They ate it when the dumplings were done and raved about how good it was. They could do nothing less; they were so hungry.

A dirt road ran between the Adamson and Skow farms. Somehow Sam and Dora's farm was always referred to as belonging to the Skows. It was good to live just across the road from Dora's folks, and for John and Mary, it was especially enjoyable after Margaret was born.

Once, when Margaret was about two years old, she decided to go to see her grandparents and toddled off through the wheat field. John was sitting on the porch when he saw a small figure emerge from among the tall stalks of grain. He went and gathered her up in his arms and carried her to the house where Mary was watching. Putting Margaret, who was enjoying the attention in Mary's arms, he said, "Here, take her!" and he turned and went toward a pile of railroad ties by the barn. He lashed two of them together and went to harness Dan, the roan he'd bought to replace Jim, the crooked-legged bay, now so long ago.

Hooking him to the ties, he flattened a path through the wheat field to Sam and Dora's so Margaret wouldn't get lost while coming to visit him and Mary.

It was about then that Sam gave Margaret the nickname of Toots, and it was Toots from then on.

Pete had married a girl named Fay Barker and lived in a sod house on a homestead he rented for a short time before moving to Havre, Montana. It left only Mil and Sam to help John and farm both places while Dora, Ella, and their mother, Mary, worked both gardens and put up many jars of vegetables, june berries, and rhubarb for the winter months. Dora picked june berries for Sam's favorite pie and the tiny sweet strawberries that grew on vines along the ground, and sometimes there would be enough for shortcake.

It snowed and blew until the drifts were as high as the porch roof and above the windows on the east side of the house. When it wasn't snowing, the sun shone, but the temperature's plummeted. Sam knocked the snow from his feet and came in. "It's fifty below out there I was going to let the cows out to drink, but the water trough is frozen solid . . . we'll have to melt the ice. Where's the washtub?"

"Hanging on the porch," Dora answered and then asked, "Did you look in on the chickens? Ma said chickens can't stand much cold, and I remember once when our chickens' combs froze. Some of them just fell off, and I felt so sorry for them."

"They were bunched up together, and I threw them a few forkfuls of hay, and they nestled right into it. Guess they're not so dumb after all. There weren't any eggs though."

It was one day when it'd started to warm up that Sam came in to say. "I'm going to take your folks into Bowbells. Your ma's worried about Thea. Do you want to go along?"

"No! I'd better not. Margaret is coughing and feels like she might have a fever."

Thea was in bed when they got there, and she threw back the covers and started to get up when she saw them, but Mary put out her hand to stop her and said, "Nei! Don't get up. I will just sit here beside you and visit."

Thea was even more pale and fragile than the last time they'd seen her, but she tried to sound encouraging as they talked and looking at Thea's sewing basket next to the bed and a stack of quilt squares, she said., "Oh my, I see you are making another quilt. It will be one of your finest."

But Thea's face flushed as she said. "Thank you, Mary, but I know it isn't. My hands are not as steady as they used to be."

Changing the subject, Mary asked, "Do you like living in town?"

"Ja! It's much less work, and Jebbe has a good job, and did I tell you the news? Jebbe has sent for my Dorthea. She will be here in a few weeks."

"Oh Thea, that is wonderful news. How did this all come about?"

"I don't exactly know. One day, he just came in and said she was coming, and I haven't been able to get anything about it out of him. He just says, 'She's coming, isn't that enough?' But I don't care. She's coming, and that is all that counts." But Thea's eyes misted over before she said, "I just wish it would have been a long time ago . . ."

Mary rose and bent to hug her sister. "Ja, I know, but it is still wonderful."

"Ja, it is, but what will I say to her?"

"You worry too much. You'll know what to say when the time comes. You won't even have to think about it, your heart will do the talking."

As John, Mary, and Sam prepared to leave, Jebbe motioned Mary aside. "I've sent for Dorthea!"

"Ya, Thea told me. I am so glad, and it was good of you to do that."

"I will have my daughter here as well!"

"Oh, I see." Mary didn't ask questions, but she wondered at his sudden interest in the daughter he'd given away as a baby when his first wife died. She would have to be eighteen or nineteen at least.

It was April before Dorthea arrived, and John and Mary were at the train depot to meet her. They watched as she stepped from the train with a valise in her hand and a frightened look on her face. There was no mistaking who she was for the resemblance to her mother was so striking. But when Mary rushed forward to embrace her, saying, "Dorthea, it is I, your Tanta Mary." The young woman shied away.

Mary immediately understood. Dorthea didn't even know her. She was a complete stranger to her, and so will her mother be when they meet.

Thea had been too weak to go to the train depot and waited nervously at home, but when Dorthea walked in, the two fell into one another's arms as if the years had washed away.

Dorthea had had the opportunity to speak with Tanta Dorthea before coming to America, so she had been told of the circumstances surrounding her and her mother's separation.

Dorthea was very kind and gentle to her mother while helping to care for Jebbe and the boys, but Thea was growing weaker. One day, when Dorthea had been there but a few weeks, her mother slipped away in her sleep.

Jebbe and the boys expected more and more of Dorthea until it was obvious to Mary that he wanted her as nothing more than a cook and housekeeper, so she and John took her home with them. It was only a few months later when Dorthea met and married Peder Duhn Pederson, a Danish immigrant who lived in Bowbells.

Jebbe's daughter had said in the beginning that when she reached twenty-one, she would leave, and that is exactly what she did.

Mary's letter to Denmark, telling of Thea's passing, was difficult to write.

> My dear Lana and all,
>
> I am sorry to have to tell you that our dear sister Thea has passed away. She went peacefully in her sleep, which I am grateful for as she was enduring much pain.
>
> As you know, her daughter, Dorthea, is here and was able to comfort her mother for those last weeks. You should have seen them when they met, hugging and crying. I can't help but wish it had been sooner as they both wished as well, but they did have that time together, which is a true blessing.

> Dorthea came to stay with us after her mother's passing for a time, but then she met and married Peder Duhn Pederson, a Danish immigrant who lives here in Bowbells. It all happened so fast, but Dorthea seems content. We call her husband simply Pete Duhn, and he calls Dorthea, Dora. Sometimes, I wonder how we ended up with so many Dortheas, Doras, and Marys in our family. You are fortunate Lana, to be one of a kind.
>
> Our love and prayers, your sister Mary

It was always difficult to avoid the questions uppermost in her mind about the war in Europe, and especially how it was affecting her native Denmark, and in particular, her brothers who had been forced into the German Army. But she didn't dare ask since she had her suspicions that letters coming from America could fall into the wrong hands and somehow be used against her family. After all, she herself had known the tyranny of that invading force for a good part of her life before coming to America. She'd seen and witnessed two separate sides: the cruel aggressive command and the ordinary, homesick young German soldiers.

* * *

It was 1914, and the war in Europe was raging, and everyone knew it was only a matter of time before the United States of America would be involved.

It had been a very long time since anyone had heard from the old country, Norway or Denmark, but Mary was thankful that Dorthea had come when she did. Any later, it might have been impossible for her to leave.

Dorthea had told them, "When I left, I was taken to Hamburg as a German citizen. Someone had gotten papers for me, and I sailed for America as soon as I got there, everything was rush, rush, rush. I was supposedly on vacation, and my return trip was scheduled on my papers, but of course, I would not return."

A few months later, the United States had entered the war and soon afterward, Mil was drafted into the army. Mary wept. "First, my brothers. And now, my son."

John was just as concerned, but he said, "I know, but he will be fighting against the German aggression. We can only pray that no harm comes to him."

Mary cried, "John, he may have to fight against his own uncles and cousins. I don't want him to go!"

John placed an arm around her, and pulling her close, he said simply, "Ja, I know. I know."

Mil was ordered to leave for a place called Fort Ord in California, and when the day arrived, everyone saw him off on the train in Bowbells. Fifteen other young men left with him, and from the windows of the train, they hung out as far as they could, grabbing the hands of family and friends until the train moved too fast to hang on.

Mil yelled, "Ma, I'll write as soon as I can. Bye, Pa. Bye, Dory." And he was gone.

There were but two short letters from Mil before he was sent aboard a ship to Europe, and then weeks went by without a word. But then a letter came, and they learned that he was safe but little else. He couldn't say where he was, only that the people there spoke French, indicating that he was nowhere near Denmark. But of course, no one knew just where his uncles were. It would be three long years before he came home—thin and haggard, but well. The memories of the war would haunt him the rest of his life, but soon after his return, he met and married May Gunther Montgomery. They would eventually move to Montana and live near Pete and Fay.

* * *

Crops had been poor, but in 1915, conditions were looking better. There had been a good snow pack in the winter, followed by frequent light rains after the fields were planted that brought the grain up and flourishing in record time. The whole spring and early summer seemed perfect.

It was a day like that when Ella came one afternoon while Dora stood at the washtub, scrubbing a pair of Sam's bib overalls on the washboard while Margaret ran about with her rag doll in one hand and her other reaching out to catch a hand full of the dog's fur with the other.

Ella was quiet. She just went to sit on the porch steps, putting her head in her hands as her elbows rested on her knees.

Dora looked up to greet her sister and then straightened her back and looked at her in expectation, but Ella said nothing. Finally, Dora asked. "Is something wrong, Ella?"

"No, I just don't feel like talking."

"Well, you can just sit there and say nothing if you want, but it looks to me like you have something on your mind."

Ella rolled her eyes up to look at her sister, and in a low voice said, "It's Ole."

"Ole? Why in the world is he on your mind?"

Ella raised her head and said, "I like him."

"Well, I like him too."

"No! I mean, that I really like him . . ."

"Ella! You don't mean . . ."

"Ya! I do."

"Ella, he is old enough to be your father. He's old enough to be my father. You can't be serious."

"I know, but I still do."

"Do you have any idea how hard it was to convince Ma and Pa to let me marry Sam because he is twelve years older than I am? Yes! You remember!"

"I know . . ." and Ella began to cry.

"Ella, does Ole know how you feel?"

"No, but . . ."

"Ella!"

But when Dora shared Ella's feelings for Ole with Sam, saying, "Can you imagine? What is she thinking?"

Sam lowered his head and scratching his ear said, "Well, I'm afraid Ole feels the same about Ella."

"No, you can't be serious."

"I'm afraid so."

"Oh my . . . what will Ma and Pa say?"

The answer was soon to come, and after much discussion, anger, and tears, Ole and Ella were married.

Late summer saw the blue flowers of flax in contrast to the gold of the wheat standing thick in the fields. No more beautiful a sight to be seen as Sam and Dora stood gazing out over their land in the early morning. It was clear and warm.

Sam had eighty acres of wheat, and just that morning, he'd gone to the field and ran his hand up a number of stalks of wheat, and catching the kernels in his hand, he blew away the chaff and found the grain ready for reaping.

The binder had seen better days, but it was all they could afford, and Sam worked most of the day to get it running. It was late afternoon by the time he was finished, but he wanted to try it out, so Dora came to help him hitch up the horses, and then watched as he made a swath around the field. He had but started when the western sky grew dark, and the wind began to blow. By the time he neared where Dora waited, it was beginning to hail. Just small wet pellets, but before they could get the team unhitched, it was hailing hard. So turning the team loose, they ran to the house and the safety of the porch where they stood holding one another and cried at the sight of their crops in ruin. The only thing salvaged was the one swath that was cut and tied. Barely enough for seed for the next year, grain for the livestock, and enough to be milled for two sacks of flour. They had so hoped for a much needed, cash crop.

The hailstorm had cut right through their fields, missing the crops of most of their neighbors, even John and Mary's fields were spared.

* * *

Dora was carrying their second child, and things looked pretty bleak with the losing of the crops, and then one day Sam came in after being to town with news. Dora always knew when he was excited about something from his silly grin.

"We'll take a drive out to the hills tomorrow."

Looking at him from the corner of her eye as she stood frying meat at the stove she said, "Sam, what is this about?"

Knowing it would do him no good to beat around the bush, Sam confessed. "There's a place that I thought we could look at."

"You mean a place to rent? Buy? Or what? It can't be to buy . . . we have no money to buy."

"Nei, Nei! It's a quarter of land that belongs to the bank, and we won't have to pay it off until we've had a crop, and a good one at that."

"But why do we have to move? We live so close to Ma and Pa and . . ."

"Look, Dory, we can't make a living on this place. There is not enough land, and there is none around to rent. I talked to John about it, and he thinks it's a good idea even though he'll miss having us near."

"Is there a house out there?"

"That is why I want to go and look at it. Come on, let's take some lunch and have a picnic." And then he called, "Toots, come on, we're going for a ride." He didn't have to say it twice.

Dora said no more, but from the look on her face, anyone could see she was not happy.

The house was not what she'd hoped for. It was a small, dilapidated shack with broken windows and a sagging porch. The barn, though bigger, was no better but there was no use trying to change Sam's mind.

He put his arm around her shoulders and squeezed her to him. "Don't worry, I'll build a new house and fix up the barn. And just look at this land."

A deal was struck with the bank, but they would remain living where they were for the time being and farm both places the first year, but right then they had another winter to get through.

There was less snow that year, but the temperatures plummeted to sixty below zero. The livestock, including the horses, had to be kept in the barn so it meant carrying water for them to drink. Sam would tie a burlap bag around a horse's nose to keep its nose from bleeding in the intense cold and after lifting a harness to its back and cinching it up, he'd hook the traces to the single tree to pull the stone boat laden with water barrels to and from the well.

The cold weather lasted way into the last of April without warming more than a few degrees.

Dora wasn't due for the baby to be born until the end of May, but her face and legs were swollen, and her back hurt. Sam insisted on doing the chores, but when he came in one day with both hands frozen, there was little else she could do but go to the barn to unharness the horse and feed the livestock. Taking her coat from the hook by the door, she started to put it on when Sam said. "Nei, I'll go back out in a few minutes. I just have to warm up."

"No, you won't! Just look at your hands. I'll bring in a pan of snow before I go to the barn. You have to thaw them out gradually."

When he sank his hands into the cold snow, he groaned, "Ooh, that hurts."

"It would hurt a lot worse if they warmed too fast," she said.

"Ya, I suppose."

She'd managed to hang the harness back on its spike in the wall and throw a forkful of hay to the cows when she felt a dull pain that lasted several seconds. After feeding the rest of the stock, Dora knew she would have to milk while she was there, so taking the pail and stool, she reached out her hand to stroke the cow's flank and setting the stool beside her udder, she sat down awkwardly, but not before another pain gripped her and then subsided. What was wrong? It was too early for the baby.

Making her way to the house, a wool hat pulled down over her ears, and the collar of her coat pulled up Dora carried the pail of milk in one hand while she held a gloved hand over her nose and cheeks. It seemed like a long way to the house, and then another pain and she stiffened and stopped, letting it pass.

At the house, Sam's hands were thawing as he sat rubbing them with the melting snow. They were splotchy red and blue, but they would be all right. When he saw her, Sam stood up and put out a hand to take the milk, but she turned it away and set it on the table.

Seeing the apprehension in her face he said, "What's wrong?"

"I feel awful. I'm having contractions, but it's way too early."

"Should I get your mother?"

"Yes! We need to get Ma. But can you go?"

"Ya, sure!" And he struggled into his coat.

Dora put a hat on his head and tied a wool scarf about his face and neck.

"Here, let me wrap your hands. Make sure you keep them in your pockets, but hurry," she said as another pain seized her.

The pains had lessened by the time Mary came, but she put Dora to bed and waited. A few more contractions, but each one decreased in intensity, and they knew it had been a false alarm.

"Oh, Ma, I thought for sure that the baby was coming, but I knew it was way too soon. Almost a month too soon."

"Sometimes this happens, having a false alarm, but you're going to be fine. You do have to get that swelling down so stay in bed with your feet up for a few days and don't eat any salt or egg whites."

Just then, the door opened and John came in with a blast of cold air. "Is Dora okay?"

Sam sat with Margaret on his lap, but when she saw her grandfather, she climbed down and ran to him, and Sam said, "Ya, it was a false alarm, but Ma put Dory to bed because her legs and face have gotten so swollen. I don't know why."

At hearing John's voice, Mary came from the bedroom and said, "We may as well go home. Dora is fine. She just needs to stay in bed for a day or so." And looking at Sam, she said, "Don't let her have any salt or egg whites."

As Mary put on her coat, John said to Sam, "I'll come in the morning to help with chores. Your hands look pretty sore. You should have had better sense. Didn't you have your gloves on?"

"Ya, but they got wet, and I was trying to hurry."

John just shook his head with a half grin.

The cold only lasted a short while longer, and then suddenly, the weather turned warm. Just in time for the Norwegian holiday, *sytten mai,* the seventeenth day of May when Norway had gained its independence from Denmark. Dora prepared *fiskefarse,* fish balls, the traditional dish for the occasion to surprise Sam. She had already learned the art of making *lefsa* from Olivia, the Norwegian flat bread made from potatoes that she would serve with it. It was, however, the last celebration of its kind in the Berg household when it was learned that Sam disliked the dish with a passion. However, lefsa remained one of the very favorite foods of the family, especially for Thanksgiving and Christmas.

It was the end of the month. the twenty-seventh of May when Dora went into labor, and she and Sam's second daughter was born. They named her Luella Marie. It was 1916.

* * *

That summer, there were many trips back and forth from the farm out on Dimond Township in the hills and the old Skow place in Bowbells Township where they'd lived since they were married. Working and seeding the fields on both farms took time, but once the seed was in the ground, and the waiting began for the grain to grow and ripen, Sam took on small carpentry jobs to sustain them.

They were still going back and forth, but Dora had set up housekeeping in the hills for when they were there, hauling cookware, bedding, and foodstuffs back and forth as the need arose.

A dry spring and the crops were spotty, but fortunately, they'd had some good rain in July, so the fields were looking better.

Sam wanted to cut hay before the wheat harvest, so they'd packed up and gone to the hills. It was before Mil and May moved to Montana, and Mil was along to help with the haying. They'd shocked most of the hay and were ready to start pitching it onto the wagon when it suddenly got very still and dark. Sam looked to the east and saw the wide, black funnel cloud as it touched the ground and move in their direction.

Yelling at Mil, he started the horses for the barn. "Mil, come on!" But Mil was already running and beat Sam to the barn and stood with the barn door open for the horses to go in.

Dora, in the meantime, had shoved a chair under the doorknob and wrapped Luella in a quilt and put her under the bed along with Margaret who didn't want to stay put.

Dora had been in the garden pulling carrots for supper when she'd felt the quiet and noticed how dark it was getting, and then she'd seen it—the tornado. She hurried inside to the children. Brownie's fur stood straight up as he yelped and dove under the porch.

When Sam reached the house, he tried the door but when it wouldn't open, he dove under the house as Mil followed.

The sound was deafening as Dora lay squeezed under the bed, holding her little ones to her as she prayed. When it was over, Dora pulled the door open and called. "Sam, Mil, where are you? Are you all right?"

When the two appeared from under the shack with cobwebs hanging from their heads, Dora couldn't help but laugh.

"What's so funny? We could have been killed. We couldn't get in the house."

"I know, but those cobwebs hanging on your heads . . . I'm sorry you couldn't get in, but I didn't see you, and the tornado was coming and . . ."

Brushing the cobwebs away, Sam said, "Nei, you did right. If you hadn't braced the door shut, the shack would have gone too." Sam pointed. "Look, the barn's gone."

Mil was already running among the debris in the yard toward the far pasture, calling, "There are the horses."

"He's right, there they are." And Sam started after him.

The horses were nervously walking in circles, pawing at the ground. It took a while before they calmed down enough for Sam and Mil to get hold of their halters to lead them back to the yard.

Dora, looking out beyond the fields, said, "I wonder where the rest of the barn is . . . and the calves?"

Sam, near tears, said, "Ya, they were still tied to the stanchion. I was going to let them go when we came from the field, but I forgot."

Dora soothed, "You can't think of everything at a time like that, Sam."

"Ya but . . ."

"Come in and have a cup of coffee, and then we'll go look."

Mil stayed with Margaret and Luella while Sam and Dora hitched the horses to the wagon and went in search of the barn debris and the calves.

The barn was scattered for a quarter of a mile, and there in a gully, they saw the two little calves. They had survived the flight and were standing with a rope around their necks, still tied to a board that had been a part of the stanchion in the barn.

A new barn was built using some boards salvaged from the barn wreckage and other materials to house a few head of young stock for the winter, and a neighbor agreed to look after them in exchange for a young steer.

Back at the place, Dora called home they learned that Ella and Ole had just had their first baby, and they'd named him Melvin.

When they went to see baby Melvin, both Anton and Annie and their two boys, Leonard and Clarence, and Christ and Olivia and their family—by now there were three: Austin, Borghild and Alfred—were all there.

Dora was glad she'd brought a frosted cake and two loaves of bread, right from the oven.

When Annie saw the cake, she threw up her hands and said, "Dory, Dory, you brought my most favorite cake. Many is the time I've tried that burnt sugar frosting, and I just can't get it right."

"It's not hard to make!" And she proceeded to tell Annie step by step how to do it.

Olivia too had brought food for lunch, so between all of them, it was a fine time. As always, the woman gathered in Ella's kitchen, and the men in the parlor while the older children played out in the barn, and the younger ones hung at their mother's knees, wanting attention or played on the floor.

October was beautiful, sunny and warm. The sunsets were even more spectacular than usual, and everyone was looking forward to the October Fest in Bowbells on Saturday. That day, most folks went to town for groceries and the like, and that day was when women gathered with women and men with men, to catch up on all the latest happenings thereabouts.

The yearly celebration meant a day of games and eating. Woman brought their very best hot dish and sometimes a ham or a roast of pork or beef, soft, wonderful buns, pies, or cakes, and several were sure to bring lefsa. Whatever the food, everyone ate until they could hold no more.

After the festivities were over and they'd picked up goods for the winter from the store and crates of supplies sent for from the Savage Company in Minneapolis, it was evening and time to start for home. After a glorious day, the feeling lingered as the wagons slowly left Bowbells under a red sky, mottled with yellow, pink, purple, and blue seeing them home.

John and Mary had been to visit Mary Inga and Charlie one Sunday afternoon and stopped at Sam and Dora's on the way home. Pulling up in the yard, Mary called out to Dora who was shelling peas on the porch.

"Your sister and Charlie have a radio. They said if you want to, you should come to listen to it."

"Did you hear the radio, Ma?"

"Ya, we did. It gives you a funny feeling, hearing somebody's voice coming from a box." Later, Dora told Sam about the radio, and they decided to go the next day.

Once they were there and seated in the Carlson parlor, Charlie took the headphones from his own head and put them on Sam, but only moments later, he took them back and put them on Dora. Moments again and he took them back to his own head, and there is where they remained until Mary Inga called them to the dining room for dinner.

On the way home, Dora said, "It was so strange to hear voices come over a wire from so far away as Minneapolis, and Charlie said that some programs come from as far away as New York, but that is inconceivable."

A letter came just after that, bringing the matter of distance ever closer as Mary read.

> Dear Mary and all,
> I hesitate to write you the news we just learned concerning our dear brother Christian, but you have the right to know. Christian has been captured and sent to Siberia, or at least this is what we have been told. I know you will pray for him as we are. We are well as I hope you are. We will keep you informed as we hear anything. We are hoping that Christian will be released soon.
> We have not seen or heard from Frederick for some time, but we do hear from Heinrick on occasion, and he has seen Frederick and says that he is well.
> As ever, Lana

Mary was not entirely surprised at the news about Christian. Somehow she had known something was wrong because no one had heard from or about him for so long. This was not characteristic of him but to actually hear it voiced was devastating.

* * *

The spring of 1917, Sam and Dora loaded the rest of their belongings into the wagon and moved out to the flats in Dimond

Township for the last time. They would continue to farm the Skow place for the time being, but they would never live there again.

When the crops and garden were in, Sam started on the new house. It was square with four rooms. The old small shack was turned into a granary, and the barn was made larger.

Krist Trastad moved to the hills shortly after Sam and Dora, so it was a frequent occurrence that one would visit the other.

When visiting Krist, he would fling the door open and say, "Come on, come on in!" with his big toothy grin and grab up whichever child was the youngest and carry her inside. Before leaving for home, they were always treated to big, thick pancakes that filled a plate and a slab of ham of equal proportions cut from a ham that he pulled from under the bed.

Krist would never fail to mention some time in Norway, involving himself and Sam and always direct it toward Sam and Dora's girls. He would begin like this: "Let me tell you about your dad . . ." When the telling was over, everyone would be wide eyed and laughing.

There was one tale in particular that he liked to tell. He would lean way back in his chair and look first at Sam who would roll his eyes as if to say, "Not again?" and then direct his attention to the girls and Dora.

"Me and Syver were herding horses up on the satre one summer, and there were two milkmaids at a farm nearby. We knew they slept in the hay mow, and Syver," nodding toward Sam, "thought it would be a fine thing to go visit them. Well, when we got there, we heard talking and laughing coming from the mow, so we knew the maids already had visitors. Well, Syver had a good idea for a prank." At this, Sam laid his head back and groaned, but Krist went on. "He . . . ," emphasizing the *he,* "moved the planks that went over the manure pit just enough to fall when anybody stepped on them. Then we hid and waited, and before long, the boys came down from the hay mow and . . . *splash*. We didn't stick around to see any more, but on our way over the hill, we caught sight of those boys brown as could be running for a nearby stream."

Margaret would sometimes say, "Dad!" And he would just grin.

Once, when Krist came to visit, he and Sam went to the slew behind the barn to cut ice. They'd saw or chop it into big chunks and haul them to the old granary where they were buried beneath mounds of straw. It would usually stay frozen long enough to make ice cream for the Fourth of July.

Krist had stepped from one ice chunk to another in an attempt to push one onto the bank when he fell head-first into the water. He refused to go change his sopping wet clothes for dry ones until that chunk was loaded and hauled to the granary.

As a result of his stubbornness, Krist came down with pneumonia and would have died, had Sam not gone to check on him after he'd insisted on going all the way home in his wet clothes.

Bill Poline went for Doc Hilts, and Krist was brought back to Sam and Dora's and put to bed where he would stay for a number of days until he insisted again on going home.

The well on the farm in the hills provided ample water for the house and livestock, but it was certainly unappealing to look at until a handful of lye was thrown in. That brought the scum and bugs to the top to be skimmed off before hauling it in barrels to the house and barn. The water was oftentimes green until it was skimmed.

Once, when Margaret was carrying a pail of water to the house before it was skimmed, a man who was looking for Sam to do some work for him drove into the yard and got out. He walked up to Margaret and asked, "What have you there?"

She answered, "Water!"

He wrinkled his nose and said, "Water! It looks terrible."

Margaret set the bucket down and took a strainer from her pocket and skimmed the scum from the water. "See? It's clear as can be."

The man asked, "Does your mother cook with it?"

Margaret tilted her head and said simply, "Sure, she boils it!"

But later, when he'd talked with Sam in the yard and was invited in for coffee, he declined and hurried off.

One day, shortly after moving to the farm in the hills, Margaret came out on the porch when she heard her grandpa's Overland car come into the yard. Expecting him to get out, she waved excitedly, but it was Aunt Ella and Uncle Ole.

Ella waved and asked, "Where is your ma?"

"Better not call her ma, she'll get mad!" Margaret replied. "Have to call her Mom or Mama!"

"Oh, I see. Well, anyway, where is she? I have something to tell her."

"She's in the field, helping dad."

Ella looked over at Ole and said, "I'll go find her."

"Nei!" he said. "I will." And he started off toward the field.

Ella went inside to make a pot of coffee, and a few minutes later, Dora came running almost out of breath.

"What's wrong with Pa?" she gasped. "Ole said he's sick."

Ella spoke softly, "Pa has rheumatic fever. He's bad! Doc Hilts is with him, and Ma sent us out to get you."

As Dora reached for her sweater by the door, she said, "Does Mary Inga know about Pa?"

"Ya, Mil and May went after her."

Sam and Ole were hurrying toward them as Ella and Dora got into the car. When Ole climbed in behind the steering wheel, Sam poked his head in through the window and said, "Dory, don't worry about anything here. We'll be in in the morning after chores." And he stepped back as the car began to move.

Dora shouted out the open window, "Don't let Toots fool with the fire or anything!"

Sam waved his hand in acknowledgement as Ole drove out to the road.

The next day, Mary insisted they should all go home after Doc Hilts assured everyone that John was not on his death bed. He had, however, suffered a great deal to his heart and had been severely weakened by the ordeal. So much so that Doc Hilts advised him to give up farming and move to town.

At this, John rose off the bed where he was to remain for several more days of recovery and shouted. "Nei! You, dumb *koff*. I cannot stop farming. This is my farm." He spoke in German.

Mary hurried to his side, saying, "John, John, hush. You will be good in no time. You will see."

But it wasn't ever good again. John found he could no longer do the work he was used to, and he finally asked Ole and Ella if they wanted to help by sharing the house and the crops, for Ole doing the work that John could no longer do.

It was agreed and Ella, who was carrying their second child, was glad to be so near her mother for when the time came for her to deliver.

And so it was that Ole, Ella, and little Melvin came to live on the homestead farm. But soon after Ella's baby was born, a little girl they named Evelyn, that John and Mary rented a house and moved into Bowbells. The winter had proven to be too much for John.

* * *

The summer of 1918, Dora delivered her and Sam's third child, a little girl they named Edna Doris, born on July 29. She was born two years, two months and two days after Luella, but she was not a happy baby, crying much of the time until it was discovered that she was being starved by nursing her mother's milk, which was lacking in the nourishment Edna needed.

Doc Hilts, who diagnosed the problem, suggested giving Edna something called Melons Food, a concoction made from different kinds of melon: watermelon, musk melon, honeydew melon, and cereal. It proved to be the very thing to stop the crying and make both Edna and everyone else content.

From that time on, anytime—anyone's child seemed out of sorts—Sam would tell them to give it Melons Food. It's too bad the Melons Food Company didn't know they had an advertising campaign going on in the hills of North Dakota.

During this time, John was in bed most of the time, and his good friend, Pete Anderson who lived in town, was a frequent visitor. The two would play cards and visit, or Pete would merely sit quietly by his bedside, sometimes reading to him or playing a tune on his guitar or violin.

John Peter Adamson passed away on January 11, 1920. He was only fifty-nine. His casket lay across two chairs in the parlor of his and Mary's rented house in Bowbells where he'd died. Mary had hoped to have it lay in the parlor of their homestead home, but the weather was far too bad with snow and ice beating against the windows to go so far. But even in the adverse weather, the house was crowded with friends and relatives of this beloved man. He was harsh at times, but never cruel, and he would do anything to help anyone. Giving of himself and his resources whenever the need arose.

John had lived a life of servitude under oftentimes cruel masters as a child, but he'd had the courage to leave it behind when he ran away, but he was never quite able to put it out of his heart. Mary would encourage him. "John, the Bible says you need to forgive the past in order to be forgiven. What good does it do to keep hatred in your heart after all these many years?"

He knew the love of a dear woman, his helpmate who was always near to encourage him and to chide him sometimes when he was too harsh. After his death, she'd light his pipe and lay it so she could smell the sweet familiar aroma, always just before retiring for the night.

Mary was called upon to deliver many babies through the years, and even now while living in Bowbells, she would be called on to help Doc Hilts with a delivery, or when he was indisposed with another case.

One night, she awoke to someone pounding on the door. Throwing back the covers and climbing out of bed, she pulled a blanket about her and went to the door. Opening it, she found a young girl standing on the porch, shivering with the cold.

The girl blurted, "My ma needs you!"

Mary pulled the girl inside while she asked, "What is wrong with your mother? Is she sick?"

"She is having a baby, but Pa says there is something awful wrong."

"Let me get dressed, and I'll come with you." And Mary hurried back to her room.

Moments later, the two were trudging through the snow to a house near the outside of town.

Opening the door, a tall, very thin man that Mary didn't recognize greeted them. "My wife, she's there in the bedroom. I'm afraid she's dying. The baby won't come."

Mary hurried toward where he pointed as she was pulling off her coat. A small, frail-looking woman lay on a bed in the corner. Her hair was stringy and wet, and her eyes were closed until a contraction forced her eyes opened in a frightened stare.

After examining the woman, Mary realized the baby was lying exactly crosswise, something she'd never seen before. There had been breech babies where a baby lay upside down and was either turned, if possible, or was born feet or buttocks first. But in this case, turning the baby was the only option, and she was unsure if she was capable to do what was necessary, but she had to try. *Where was Doc Hilts?* she wondered. He should be here, but when she'd asked, the man had said, "The Doc was out of town."

When another contraction came, she told the woman, "Don't push! I have to turn the baby." But it was something she would not have had to say, for the woman was too exhausted to do otherwise.

Mary couldn't tell in which direction the head lay until she felt the small shoulder, and pushing brought it and the head down. Now if only the woman had the strength to push the baby out. Another contraction and Mary shouted, "Now push!" and the woman responded with every ounce of strength she possessed. And it was done. It took a few good taps on the baby's bottom, but then the baby girl let out a lusty cry. The baby's name was Anna Lindquist.

* * *

This was not a good time. John had so recently passed away, and then two letters came. One from Norway, and one from Denmark both bearing sad news. They read as follows:

> My dear brothers,
>
> I am sending this post to our brother Syver since it is the most recent address that I have. This is to notify you of our Mor's passing. Far buried her in the cemetery between Boyetraet and Mjondalen, he carved a marker and carried it on foot all that way to her grave. Most of us, her children left in Norway, were privileged to see her before her passing but not all. She often spoke of all of you in America, and I know it was your dreams to return to see her, but be assured that she knew that. Far is well.
>
> Your brother, Johannes

Sam was so devastated about the news of his mother's passing that he simply handed the letter to Dora and walked toward the open field where the hay rake sat. Climbing to the seat, he buried his face in his hands and wept. He was there for a long while before Dora went to comfort him. All he said was "I always thought to go home to see her . . ."

The next day, Dora accompanied him to Anton's and then to Ole's to share the sad news of the letter. Anton said he would reach Ed in Minneapolis. Only Ed had been back to Norway and then, a long time before.

The other letter came but a few weeks later.

My dearest Mary,

    I regret to tell you that our dear brother Christian has died. He was being sent back to Denmark from Siberia when he died en route. He was in very poor condition, so it is truly a blessing that he need not suffer any longer. We have buried him next to our mor and far. We will not see his smiling face until we rejoice with him in heaven. I will write to you again soon.

Your sister, Lana

When the letter came about Christian, there was only Anna to tell, and Mary waited a few days to deal with her own grief before going to share it with her sister Anna. She hadn't seen her since John's funeral, so it was about time she visited her anyway. She would ask Sam and Dora to take her the next Sunday after church.

Anna and Ole Rose were glad to see them, and Anna hurried to put on a pot of coffee. Mary wondered to herself why it was that they always called him that instead of just, Ole and then dismissed it from her mind.

Ole asked Sam to join him on the porch since Anna didn't like him to smoke his cigar in the house, and as they talked, Dora went to supervise the children, all cousins to one another. Mary and Anna sat at the table to catch up, but after a few moments of small talk Mary said, "I'm afraid I've come with bad news."

"Oh my, what has happened now?"

Mary pulled Lana's letter from her pocket, but before she handed it to Anna, she said, "I'm afraid Christian has died."

The two sat in silence for a moment, just looking at one another in disbelief.

Wet eyed, Anna turned her attention to the letter. When she was through, she laid it on the table and said, "It's hard to believe. Of all of us, he was always so gentle and kind. Whenever I think of him, he is always smiling."

"I know, but as Lana says in her letter, 'we'll see his smiling face when we rejoice with him in heaven,' but it is so hard to believe that he is gone."

* * *

During this time in the early '20s, Ole and Ella moved from the homestead farm, and Mary sold the homestead to the William Quanbeck family.

Mary bought a small house in Coteau, a town six miles northwest of Bowbells and had the house moved on to a vacant lot. One of the first nights she lived there, Luella stayed with her, and it started to rain. It rained and rained, and the roof began to leak. One leak was right over the bed, and there was nowhere to move the bed, so they gathered up the covers into a pile and put Mary's big black umbrella over them. Luella sat huddled among the covers while Mary went about placing kettles beneath other leaks. By the next day, the rain had stopped and Sam came to repair the roof.

The school in the hills was closed when the district could no longer afford a teacher, so Sam and Dora rented a house in Coteau for the winter. Margaret could then go to school, and Dora, who was carrying her fourth child, could be near her mother for the baby's birth.

There was a blizzard the night Dora went into labor. It had been so nice during the day that Sam went out to the farm to see how things were going, but first he'd brought Dora's mother to stay with her while he was gone.

A New Beginning

When the storm hit, Dora worried that Sam might get caught out in it, but he'd seen it coming and stayed on at the farm, knowing that Mary was with Dora and the girls.

When at last the baby, Alice Leona, was born, Dora cradled her in her arms and didn't care one bit that she wasn't the boy they had hoped for. It was January 26, 1921.

It was two days before Sam made it home, and he knew the baby had come even before he went into the house. He could hear a baby's cry and somehow knew it was a girl because when he opened the door, he said, "Is she all right?"

Until the school in the hills was reopened, Margaret and Luella would stay in Coteau with their grandmother, Mary, during the winter.

When the school in the hills reopened, a young woman named Jennie Eckberg was hired to be the teacher. Miss Eckberg boarded with Sam and Dora, and it was then they bought a chemical toilet. Sam built a small room inside to house the toilet, and everyone was happy to not have to use, the outhouse when it was cold. The stiff paper from the Sears Roebuck catalog was still used as toilet paper, but instead of being dropped down the hole of the outhouse, it had to be placed in a covered can next to the toilet, even the soft red tissue paper, individually wrapping the apples they had bought in the fall and used as toilet paper.

Dora heard about people trapping muskrat and gophers, and she suggested the idea to Sam. "Wilma Orstead said her boy was getting $1.35 for every muskrat hide and 5¢ for every gopher's tail and front feet. Maybe you should start trapping once in a while."

Sam was sitting at the table holding a teaspoon full of sugar in one hand and his other about a cup of hot coffee and ready to put the sugar in his mouth, a common practice for him, when he would wash the sugar down with the coffee. A bit startled by Dora's suggestion, he hurriedly put the sugar in his mouth and almost choked on the coffee before he said, "Ya? Them little devils don't do any harm, do they?"

"Sam, you know they do, or nobody would want to get rid of them."

"Well, let those guys trap 'em then."

"You're just a scardey-cat." She grinned.

"Nei, I don't like to kill anything."

"Ya, I know," she soothed.

But that was not the end of it. Later, Sam noticed how many hills of dirt the gophers had raised when he was in the field with the binder. It caused a lot of dirt to get mixed in the feed and seed grain. And then, if that was not enough, he found a muskrat helping itself to a feast in the grain bin.

That same evening when he came from the field, he hung his brimmed hat on the chair post, leaving an indentation in his sweaty dark hair of the hat on his forehead. And said, "Ya, I got to get rid of those gophers, and I just found one of them muskrats in the grain bin havin' a high old time."

Dora grinned, "You going to run after them or get 'em with traps?"

All Sam said was "ya, ya."

A neighbor, Bill Poline, brought Sam some traps he wasn't using, and Sam got them placed.

The very next morning, the traps were full, but that was when the trouble began. Sam couldn't bring himself to kill the ones that were still alive, so he'd let them escape.

Margaret saw what he was doing and offered to do the killing. She said, "It's easy, just wring their necks, but then they might bite, so just knock 'em in the head." So from then on without discussion, it was her job.

Then in the late fall, Sam went to check the traps and found a frozen muskrat. Bringing it home, he asked Luella to hold the tail to make it easier to skin, but the moment he began, the critter came to life, and Luella squealed and let go of the tail, and it jumped to the ground and was gone in a flash. Sam shivered, and that was the end of the trapping.

It was still later that winter when Sam came home from a neighbor's and missed Brownie, the family's dog. He had always been there at the end of the drive waiting for him. Going in the house, he asked, "Have you seen Brownie?"

Dora looked up from peeling potatoes. "No! I had some scraps for him earlier, but he didn't come when I called. I suppose he's off chasing rabbits."

"Ya, he must be."

In the afternoon, the dog hadn't come home, and Sam decided to go look for him.

It was turning dark when Sam came up on the porch carrying Brownie. He had gotten caught in a neighbor's trap on some land that Sam had rented and the leg that was caught in the trap was crushed and frozen.

Dora hurried and laid a worn sheet blanket on the table, and Sam laid Brownie on it.

"Poor Brownie!" Edna said with tears running down her face as she patted the dog's thick brown fur.

"Ya, but we'll fix him up." Dora sounded more confident than she was as she wrapped the injured leg and foot.

The following week, it was clear that Brownie would lose a part of his leg, but it didn't prevent him from getting around almost as good as he had before.

One evening, when the spring seeding was done in the fields and the garden planted, Sam and Dora sat on the steps of the porch reminiscing.

Dora smiled. "I was just thinking about the day Margaret made muffins, and I came in from the field and sat down and ate every last one of them. I didn't know the kids hadn't had any, and then I saw Toots starting to cry. I felt bad, so I brought in wood, so she could make more the next day, and wouldn't you know she must have made a double batch because the whole table was full of them. She couldn't have been more than eight."

"Ya," Sam said, "for such a little tyke, she was a big help, and she still is . . . I can still see her when you'd tie Edna in the rocking chair, and Toots would stand washing dishes at the pan and rocking with her foot at the same time."

Dora laughed. "And remember when we got all those baby chicks, and so many of them died? I never could figure out why they died. It never happened before or after, not that many anyway. But remember the cemeteries the kids made when they would bury the white ones in the Protestant cemetery, and the black ones in the Catholic cemetery?" Then looking at Sam, she said, "I could never figure out why the distinction between the black ones and the white ones and one being Protestant and the other Catholic."

They were quiet in their thinking back for a little while, and then Dora said, "But it hasn't always been so funny either. Luella sure got a good spanking when she cut up the quilt I'd just made."

"I don't remember that," he said.

"Oh, you never like to remember any thing they did wrong." And they grinned at one another.

"You know how I tie the quilts? Well, she held every tie and cut it out . . . clear through to the other side."

"Oh ya!" he said

"And, Alice, when she found the kittens in the hay and came carrying them in her arms and pockets with the mother cat following right on her heels. I remember how she cried when we told her she had to take them back. Poor little things didn't even have their eyes open yet. I think Edna helped to take them back to the hay."

Their time of reminiscing came to an abrupt end when there was a sudden crack of lightning and a loud roll of thunder and it began to rain.

* * *

Ole had gotten a card from Anna's daughter. Anna was their sister who they discovered lived in Washington State, in a town called Everett. They knew that Fritjof Eriksen, her husband, had come to Montana, and Anna and their four children—Merit (Helen), Astrid (Easter), Magnhild (Mildred), and Finn—had followed in 1912, but no one knew where they were, only that they had lived for some time, somewhere in Montana, and then moved west.

Anna too was not at all sure where her brothers were, only that they had funded her trip to America while living somewhere in the Dakotas at a place with bells as part of the name.

It was Fritjof and Anna's daughter, Mildred, who finally tried to find them. She wrote a postcard saying,

Ole, if you get this card, please write to me. Are you married?

Your sister's daughter, Mildred

Mildred addressed the card to Ole Berg, Bluebells, South Dakota.

The card was mailed shortly before Christmas, and after a journey through the Dakotas and passing through a number of hands, it finally reached Ole in Bowbells, North Dakota. It was now the end of May.

It was Ella who answered the card, and answering Mildred's question, she wrote the following:

"Yes, Ole is very much married. We just had our fifth baby."

By then, Ole and Ella had Melvin, Evelyn, Gordon, Oliver, and Henry. And from that first postcard, a correspondence developed between all of the Berg families and the Eriksen family out in Everett, Washington.

In June, the crops looked good, and Sam was able to spend a little time in the workshop he'd built adjacent to the granary. During the winter, he'd built a large cabinet. It had three drawers across the bottom, all intricately carved. Across the top were shelves for china with beautiful carving across the top and down the sides. Now that the weather had turned warm, he could put on its coats of shellac.

He'd spend hours in the winter drawing carving patterns and sketching furniture, and animals and even people in the leather-bound sketchbook, he'd brought from Norway.

His talent was evident in many of the buildings in Bowbells. His talent had first shown itself through his father in Norway and in several of his brothers, especially Ole and Johannes. He'd thought that one day he might have a son to carry it on, but now when he saw what his girls were capable of, he wondered why he needed sons.

Sam and Dora took a few moments one early morning before the fall work began to feel the soft warmth of the early sun, and the stir of a breeze on their faces as they walked up the hill behind the house to look out over their fields.

Sam bought a threshing outfit about this time, a steam engine and a big wooden separator, and was glad they had three such nice teams. Jim and Barney, and Dave and Dolly were big, perfectly matched teams, while Beauty and Wilson were bay Morgans and used strictly for pulling the buggy or other light loads.

Beauty was Dora's riding horse and her pride and joy. When Sam suggested that the team could possibly help in the threshing Dora hit the roof. "I should say not!"

"I thought they could pull a cook car," he said.

"A cook car? We don't have a cook car, and besides, it would be too heavy for them."

"I was thinking to get one. You could cook, and it would mean more money for us."

"Well, I guess I could, if Ma would come out to stay with the kids, but we'll have to pull it out to wherever you're threshing with Jim and Barney. Who has a cook car they want to sell anyway?"

"Maynard Goodyjohn! It'll need some cleaning, and maybe a little work hasn't been used for a long time."

"Well, all right then. See what he wants for it."

The next day, Sam pulled into the yard with a cook car that had seen better days. And they set to work getting it ready.

Inside were benches along the front sides of the car with a Monarch cook stove and cupboards. Just inside the door was a table built against the wall with two sleeping bunks lying flat against the wall that would be let down for sleeping at night, a box for coal sat by the stove and a barrel for water next to it, an assortment of kettles hung on the wall.

When the time came, both Maynard and Bill Poline came with their wagons to help. The others were mostly transients that followed the harvest.

Once at the field where they were to be, sometimes several miles from home, they'd get set up to start the next morning at dawn. The hayracks were loaded with bundles and stood ready to be spike pitched into the hopper of the thresher.

The cook car was, however, put into immediate use. The fire in the stove was started and the water for coffee put on to heat. That first evening they would have ham sandwiches, baked beans, potato salad, and cake and just let the first man complain.

Dora had already baked for days to be ready, hardtack and cookies, anything that would keep without being cooled. And then the day before she'd baked bread, rolls, pies, and cake. This would all help for the first day. Only the hot food would need to be prepared.

Dora expected her helper to be there at daybreak, but when she didn't come, Dora flew into the task of getting the hot breakfast that was expected ready. Bacon, eggs, fried potatoes, fried ham, pancakes, and bread. *That should do it*, she thought.

After breakfast, they finished greasing the machinery, and put the belt between the steam tractor and the threshing machine and started her up.

The day began as the men spike pitched the bundles into the hopper, and the grain began to appear from the long spout into the first empty wagon. At the same time, the straw flew from the other side into a pile.

Three of the men to help in the harvest were transients who came year after year. They could always expect them around the first part of July. Jimmy was maybe in his forties and must have come from the south, the way he drawled. He was neat as a pin, but Harry, on the other hand, looked like he'd never seen enough water to get wet. Clancy came up from the black hills and never had much to say, but all three were good workers and honest, something Sam appreciated since honesty and hard work was what he lived by.

The rest of the crew unfortunately was not always the best caliber of men. Some of them were members of the IWW, International Workers of the World, a transient and often radical group who followed the harvests, sometimes using threats of sabotage to the threshing operation if their demands were not met. They were said to have burned fields of wheat all the way from the eastern part of Washington State throughout the Midwest and further east. Burning granaries where wheat was stored as well. The purpose being to sabotage America's war effort during the war against German aggression in Europe, when thousands of American troops fought throughout Europe. And now, after the war, to impose their hatred of America for siding against Germany.

The IWW was made-up mostly of Germans who had sympathized with Germany during the war and other radical groups who generally didn't know or care what the purpose was. They only relished causing trouble.

The whole thing—the IWW, the war with Germany—had greatly affected the good upstanding people of German heritage living in America, emigrants as well as naturalized American citizens, but especially those who spoke using the German language.

Such a family had been the Adamsons. Though being Danish, but with the German language being used more than Danish, when not struggling with English, the language of

America. It was then and especially when their own son, Emil (Mil) went off to war to fight the Germans that German was no longer spoken in their home or anywhere else.

Sam, of course, had heard of the IWW, but hadn't encountered any of them until the third year of his threshing operation. It was Clancy from the black hills country who came to him about it. Clancy was tall and lanky and didn't have a lot to say as a rule, but when he did, it meant something.

The day he arrived, he went to Sam and confided, "Mr. Berg, I want to warn you about something."

"Good to see you, Clancy. Warn me about what?"

Clancy took off his hat and slowly smoothed his hair with his hand, before saying, "There's a bunch of fellas headin' up this way. They're part of the IWW, and I'd advise you not to hire 'em on. I'd tell 'em you already got your crew."

"I've heard of them, and it wouldn't be a lie to say I've got my crew because I have. Thanks for telling me, Clancy. You better go on up to the cook car and have some pie and coffee. I think its june berry."

Gunda Nelson's daughter, Borghild, came to help Dora in the cook car the next day, but Sam would bring Margaret to help until Gunda Nelson could come herself.

When Margaret got there, Dora asked, "How is everything at home?"

Margaret wrinkled up her nose, and said, "Lue found this old smelly straw tick and got Edna to lie on it and cut out a dress by cutting around her. But Gradma got after her when she found her trying to sew it on the sewing machine."

Dora shook her head. "Oh my . . . that girl."

"She got two dresses out of it, if you could call them dresses," Margaret added.

Sam had brought Margaret in the car. It was a model-T with side curtains. He'd driven it rather than the team and wagon since Delmar Johnson, one of the hands, was interested in buying it.

If the car was sold, Sam could then buy the new car they had been wanting, and it seemed as though the young man and Sam had struck a bargain for a time when the harvest season was over, but for now, he would take Margaret (Toots) home in the car and bring back the wagon and team.

Gunda Nelson was a welcome sight when she entered the cook car ready to work. She was stout and only a little over five feet in her early thirties.

As she came in, she almost shouted, "I am Gunda! Ufta, it is hot."

"It's hot all right. Can you bake a good pie?" Dora asked.

"Ya, I make good pies," she said.

"Good! We'll need four apple pies and two june berry. Better make that three june berry. You better get started right away. You'll find the dried apples in that cupboard and the canned berries in a box outside. Here's the flour and lard."

It was crowded for two women to work, and it wasn't until the bread was set to rise for the mornings, baking that the two bunks could be let down from the wall for a few hours of sleep. In the morning, the cooking and baking would start all over again as the threshing outfit moved from farm to farm.

The threshing had just begun at the second farm when a group of tough-looking men came up to the door of the cook car. Dora knew they were not part of the crew and asked, "What is it you want?"

"We're signin' on!" said the gruffest of the lot.

Dora with a voice of authority said, "Well, I'm sorry, but we already have a crew."

"Is that so?" said the man. "Where's the boss?"

Dora wanted to say, *I'm one of the bosses, and get outa here,* but she held her tongue and said, "He's in the field."

"I'll go hire on while you feed these fellas."

"It's not time for dinner, and I don't think you'll be hired."

"Give 'em something. We're about starved. I'll be right back."

As much as Dora didn't want to, she did feel a pang of guilt. The men standing outside the door craning their necks to look in at the food looked like they hadn't eaten for a month of Sundays.

"All right, go sit in the grass, and I'll bring you something." But Gunda was way ahead of her. She'd already poured four cups of coffee and sliced and buttered a half a loaf of bread. She said as she handed Dora the plate of bread to carry out, "I knew you'd feed 'em. I'll carry the coffee."

When Sam said he wasn't hiring, the man went for his pocket. But before he had the chance to pull anything from it, the other men on the crew circled around, and Clancy said, "I wouldn't do that if I were you."

After looking at the men, he'd have to fight if he pursued the matter, the stranger turned and walked back toward the cook car with Sam and the others right behind him.

At the cook car, he said, "Come on, let's get outta here." And the other four men got up from where they were seated, swallowed the last of their coffee, and stuffed the last of the bread into their mouths and followed. It was the last they were seen around there, but it was heard they'd caused trouble a few miles south.

The heat seemed to be suffocating, especially in the cook car, but then it started to rain and the threshing had to stop, but the men still had to eat. It would be weeks before they could finish the threshing and go home.

* * *

The winter months were creeping up, so the day after finishing their own harvest, when the hay was in the barn and the barrels of grain ground, a young steer was butchered. The day was spent cutting the meat and making blood sausage.

The next day meant canning the meat before it spoiled.

Luella was put to washing jars while Dora and Margaret cut the meat in chunks to fill them.

All the while, a big canning vessel of water was heating on the cook stove, and Dora carefully put the filled and sealed jars in the canner to cook.

Edna played with Alice and tried to keep her out of the way of the busy kitchen, but Alice was not cooperating. Edna called, "Mom, Alice won't mind."

Dora stopped what she was doing, and wiping her hands on her apron, she took Alice by the arm and said, "Now listen here, you pay attention to what your sister tells you. Do you hear?" and then to Edna, "Why don't you take her outside to play?"

Edna, looking more than a little disgusted with her sister, said, "All right," and dragged Alice down the stairs of the porch.

It was late afternoon when the canning was put to rest until after supper, and Sam heard his name called to come in to eat. As he washed his hands in the pan on the porch, he happened to look toward the barn and saw smoke coming from the loft. At first, he thought he was seeing things. After all, he'd just come from there, but then he knew and he hollered, "Dory, the barn is on fire!"

Dora dropped what she was doing, grabbed a pail, and said to the girls on the way out the door, "Stay in the house! Don't come out! Do you hear?" But she didn't wait for an answer. She followed Sam at a run and entered the barn. They quickly chased the horses and calves from the burning barn and let the two cows standing in stanchions, waiting to be milked, loose and slapped their backsides, yelling, "Git! Git!"

They tried in vain to squelch the flames that were spreading rapidly. Sam grabbed the top of a barrel of ground grain to drag it out, but before he could move it, flames licked at his outstretched arm, and he had to leave it and run.

Once again, Sam and Dora had to stand and watch yet another disaster, as they held one another and cried. A pathway of burned grass led from a neighbor's farm. A cigarette? Perhaps!

There was little they could do until spring so Sam put up a makeshift barn into the side of a hill. There was barely enough room for the cows and a team of horses. Beauty and Wilson would stay, and he would ask Christ if he would have room for the other two teams and maybe some calves. He would offer some of the calves in exchange for the horses keep.

In the meantime, he'd have to haul in enough hay and grain for the winter from somewhere. He'd have to see if anyone had any for sale or maybe trade.

Coming home with a load of hay from the Sorensons, Sam announced, "Knute and Maude are having a house party Saturday night. Maude said to bring whatever you want to eat. She's making a cake and ham sandwiches."

The excitement mounted as the week went by with everyone looking forward to the music and dancing. The anticipation eased the remembrance of the burning barn.

The Sorenson house was not large by any means, but large enough that when the night came and the furniture was pushed back, there was room for dancing.

The food was put on a table in the corner, and coats and quilts were laid on the floor beneath it for the little ones to lie on.

Soon, other neighbors arrived, and the fun began.

Nathan Moe brought his accordion, and Marge carried in a bowl of potato salad.

Dave and Cora Heikle came with their instruments. Dave was quite good on the banjo, but Cora left a lot to be desired as she drew the bow over the strings of the violin. So much so that Ben Ness excused himself from his wife, and taking the violin from Cora's hands, he handed it to Krist and said, "Come on, Cora, you can't miss this polka." And he whirled her to the center of the room while Krist hid the violin out of sight. Taking turns, the men who were present kept Cora away from her violin for the rest of the evening.

Any of the children old enough to dance, and that included most of them over five years old, were allowed to stay up. The others were put to bed, lying across a bed or beneath a table or bench to be safe from dancing feet.

It was late and time to go home when it was discovered that snow was falling heavily and the wind was picking up, and everyone was forced to spend the night at the Sorensons.

There were not enough beds or quilts for everyone, and they'd run out of coal for the fire.

Some old leather horse collars were brought from the barn and cut up small enough to burn, but oh, what a smell! The smell was almost worse than the cold.

Some of the adults and older children agreed to stay up and play cards to pass the time.

By the time morning came, the sky was bright and blue and the snow that lay yet unmarred by footprints or animal tracks shimmered in the sun.

* * *

The thawing ground was like honeycomb the day Dora took Beauty to find a cow that hadn't come in for milking. She'd found the cow mired in mud by the slew and was going home to get help when all of a sudden a neighbor's bull came charging. In an attempt to get out of its way, Beauty turned a somersault with Dora on her. Dora heard her collarbone break when she hit the ground.

Beauty got to her feet, and Dora managed to mount, and grabbing a handful of mane, she whispered, "Easy, girl, you have to take me home."

The bull seemed to have disappeared; it was nowhere in sight.

At the house, she went inside and peeled her muddy clothes into a pile on the floor as the girls gathered around, wanting to know what had happened. "The neighbor's bull came at us, and Beauty took a somersault with me on her, and I must have broken my collar bone, but I'll be fine." She asked Margaret, "Will you pour me some water, so I can wash this mud off?" And looking at Luella, she said, "Do you think you could go for Maynard or Bill? Bess is stuck in the mud by the coulee!"

As Lu put her coat on, Edna asked, "Can I go too?"

"Yes, go ahead. Lu, wait for your sister."

"Toots, get the doctor's book. It'll show how to bandage my shoulder."

After reading the instructions, she told Margaret to tear four-inch strips from an old bed sheet and wrap them about her shoulder and body.

"Do you think you can do that?"

"I'll try."

A short while later, Dora's shoulder was wrapped beneath a clean housedress, and when Sam came in for supper, Dora acted as if nothing had happened.

When Edna accidentally drank kerosene the next week, Doc Hilts was called, but she was all right by the time he got there because Dora had gotten her to vomit. While he was there, Dora told him about her collarbone, and when he saw the bandage, he laughed. "Good job, Toots." Margaret beamed.

It was that same spring when Sam started walking funny, and Dora asked him what was wrong. At first, he denied that anything was wrong, but it wasn't long before he couldn't hide that he was in terrible pain.

Dora sent Margaret on horseback to Bill Poline's who was the closest neighbor to come and drive them to the doctor.

By the time Bill came, Sam was throwing up and white as a sheet. Bill opened the door of his car as Sam came with Dora down the porch steps.

"You don't look so good, Sam!"

"I don't feel so good either!"

Doc Hilts was at his office when they got there and took one look at Sam and said, "Up on the table, Sam, and let's have a look at you."

Moments later, he turned to Dora. "I have to operate and right now."

"What's wrong with him?"

"His appendix, and I hope it hasn't burst."

Dora turned white, and said, "Oh my . . ."

Sam moaned from the table. "What is it?" Doc Hilts repeated the diagnosis, leaving out the "burst" part.

While he helped Sam out of his clothes, Doc Hilts spoke quietly to Dora. "You'll have to assist me. Mrs. Berget is out of town visiting her sister."

"Me?" she whispered. "What can I do? I've never—"

He didn't let her finish. "You'll do just fine, but first, tell Bill to go after Simon Halverson. He'll have to give the anesthetic."

"But he's a dentist."

Grinning, he said, "Dentist, doctor, veterinarian, what's the difference?" And then, he added, "He does it for me all the time."

Once Sam was asleep, the surgery began. At first, Dora thought she was going to pass out but as time went on, and she did what she was told. She became interested in the procedure until Doc Hilts said, "Oh my, this isn't good!"

Frightened, Dora exclaimed, "Why, what's wrong?"

"His appendix is attached to his spine."

"What does that mean?"

"It means that I have to be mighty careful of his spinal cord, and there are so many nerves to deal with."

He looked at the dentist. "How's he doing?"

"Good. His heart rate is right up there, and his breathing is fine."

"We'll have to keep him under a while longer." And Simon agreed.

"Good, well here goes." And he took what looked like a small paring knife and asked Dora for a clamp.

At this point, Dora was feeling panic, and Doc looked up at her. "This is no time to get squeamish." But he could see the tears welling up in her eyes.

"It'll only be another minute or two, and we'll have it. Will you be all right?"

"Yes!" she said firmly, and he proceeded.

When it was over, he told Dora. "A fraction of an inch, and I might have cut a nerve, and he could have been paralyzed. Just a fraction of an inch." And he wiped the sweat from his forehead and sat down.

Sam was laid up for a time, but not as long as he was told to. He had things to do, and one Morning, he got up and just got dressed. As he placed his hat on his head; Dora looked up from cooking breakfast and asked, "Just where do you think you are going?"

"To the barn. I've laid around long enough."

"But Doc Hilts said—"

"I don't care what he said. I feel fine, and I'm going to the barn."

"All right, go then, but don't go lifting on anything." And then asking, she said, "Don't you want some breakfast before you go out?"

"Ya!" And he hung his hat on the chair post and sat down at the table with the girls while Dora dished up their plates with fried potatoes and ham.

Alice wrinkled her nose at what was put on her plate, and Margaret said, "Big baby!"

But when Alice started to cry, Sam soothed, "Nay, nay, just eat your ham then." And immediately, Alice stopped crying and wiped her eyes after giving Sam an adoring look.

When Dora gave him a look that said, "She's got you right around her finger," Sam quickly changed the subject and said, "I think we better get the new barn built as soon as I finish seeding."

"That's right. Carl Carlson said he'd help, didn't he?"

"Ya! He's coming to help me finish the seeding tomorrow. That's why I've got to get everything ready so we can get an early start. Then we'll get started on the barn."

Dora could say so much with just one look, and he answered it with. "I'll have Carl ride the drill. Don't worry, I'll be careful."

The barn was larger than the one that had burned. It was complete with a full loft with stairs going up instead of a ladder and the loft floor was smooth. When it was complete, some of the neighbors talked Sam and Dora into having barn dances.

The dances, however, would have to wait until after the harvest, butchering, canning, and other preparations for another coming of winter.

When the time came to take the threshing outfit to the first farm to harvest, it was Dora who drove to get her mother to stay on the farm with the girls. Margaret insisted that she was perfectly capable of taking care of things, but Sam and Dora knew she would be in danger of a mutiny. It would take their grandmother to keep things going smoothly while Dora went to cook in the cook car.

* * *

The new automobile they'd bought just after the barn was built proved to be one that Dora could drive without having to crank it to get it started and then run to get in and get her foot on the gas pedal before it died. A challenge she had long given up, but now, it was not unusual to see her bouncing across the fields on her way to somewhere.

The gas-operated washing machine stood filled with hot soapy water and a load of dirty clothes, but the engine wouldn't start. Dora knew what was wrong. The spark plug was worn out and she would have to change it, but how? She'd used the last one she had. Then she thought of the automobile. There were spark plugs in it. Without hesitation, she hurried out and lifting the hood, she removed a spark plug and returned to the washing machine and replaced the old one and the machine started on the first try.

Sam came from the barn and hollered over the sound of the washing machine. "Dory, I'm going to town for a part for the binder."

"Wait! Let me give you a small list. I need a few things for baking."

"Do you want to go along?"

"No, I'm washing clothes."

Sam started for town with the automobile chugging and missing. Thinking it was probably some water in the gas tank that would dissipate as he went along, he paid it little mind until it got worse and not better. By the time he stopped to look under the hood and found that the engine was missing a spark plug, he was already closer to town than home so he endured the ride and went on. It was hours before he would get home.

Storming into the house, he asked, "What did you do with the spark plug? I had to buy a new one in town. I hardly made it in, it was missing so bad. When I left for town, it didn't sound too good, but it was moving right along and then it started to spit and sputter."

Dora's face turned red. "Oh, I forgot to tell you. I had to use it for the washing machine."

All he could do was groan.

Once the threshing outfit and the cook car came back to the Berg farm and finished the harvest there, the threshing crew gathered their bedrolls and knapsacks from the barn where they stayed during the harvest and left for the season.

Dora had waited for their departure, so she could gather the straw they'd slept on to burn. She stacked it in the barnyard and lit a match to it.

Finding lice in Alice's hair when she kept scratching her head, Dora had no choice but to douse Alice's head with kerosene. Alice liked to go to the barn to listen to the stories the men from the threshing crew told and had been scolded time and again about doing so, warned that sometimes some of the migrant crew carried lice in their hair and clothing. It wasn't until the horror of knowing she had lice herself that she learned a good lesson because she never again entered the barn when the thresher crew was there, nor did she ever get anywhere near them, in the barn or otherwise.

It was the end of September before the first dance was held in the Berg's barn. Everyone from the hills came, including those with instruments. Jens Larson called the square and circle dances, and everyone had a good time. But when it became apparent that some of the men were going out to their cars for a swig or two or more of liquor the barn dances soon came to an end.

Edna started school that year, leaving Alice, the only child at home, during the day. Alice loved the room just inside the door called the vestibule. The name vestibule seemed so elegant to her that she spent hours there, pretending that she was a princess as she played having tea and cakes with her rag doll. The princess was the character in a book Dora was reading out loud in the evenings before bedtime.

Dora was never fond of her name. She would have denied that it was because of it being the name of her sister who had died so sadly, but Mary knew better. Not that Dora held any bad feelings toward the sister she never knew, but secretly she wished she'd been given a name of her own.

The girls didn't realize this of course, only that their mother didn't like her name, so in fun they would chant "Dora Amelia Tora Adamson Berg" over and over, driving her crazy. How glad she was when they outgrew the game.

Naming a child for one who had died was a custom Mary regretted ever existed, and on more than one occasion when she delivered a baby to a couple who had previously lost a child and they were about to name the baby by the same name, she would speak up and let her feelings be known on the matter, using Dora as an example and sometimes changing their mind.

* * *

It was about this time in 1925 when Sam sold the threshing outfit and cook car. The school in the hills had once again closed its doors, and Sam and Dora decided to rent a house in Bowbells so the girls could attend school. Mary, who was not feeling well, was asked to come to live with them, so she sold her place in Coteau and Sam brought her to Bowbells. He was as much a son to her as Dora was a daughter.

Sam tried going back and forth to the farm the next spring to get a crop in and still take on building projects in town, but finally at the end of June they went back to the farm.

The school in the hills opened once more, but the teacher, Miss Abernathy left to be married just after Christmas, and no one else applied for the position, so Sam and Dora and the girls moved once again back to Bowbells.

Sam bought a large lot near the ballpark in Bowbells and found a building to move on to it. It was merely a shell, so he went to work digging a basement and building a foundation beneath before closing it in.

In the meantime, a man named Dalymare who had inherited a farm just outside of Bowbells needed someone to take care of the livestock since he lived in Minneapolis. Sam and Dora took the job and lived there while Sam worked on the house in town. Dora and Margaret milked the cows and separated the cream from the milk, fed most of the milk to the pigs, and sold the cream. It was Luella and Edna's job to wash the many parts of the cream separator and carry the milk to the pigs and help to clean the barn.

There was the barn and pig house to clean and cattle to feed, so when Carl Carlson came by one day, they persuaded him to stay to help.

Sam would sometimes have one of the girls go with him to keep the fire going in the house in town, so the plaster he'd troweled onto the walls would dry. One day, Luella was along to tend the fire when she discovered four chests of drawers that Sam had built in a shed. There was one large, two medium-sized, and one small one, and Luella knew her dad had built them for her sisters and herself. Sam tried to convince her that they were for another family in town, but he couldn't fool her, so he finally swore her to secrecy. "Now don't go telling your sisters! You'll spoil the surprise. I built them for when we move into the house."

That seemed to satisfy her, and she promised. "I promise I won't tell." And if there was anything Luella could do it was to keep a secret, but she didn't leave it at that, asking, "What color are you going to paint them?"

Sam looked her right in the eye and had only one word to say, "Luella!" And she knew she was treading on dangerous ground and said no more. But what that dangerous ground might have been is anyone's guess since Sam was certainly not the disciplinarian.

That winter, Sam built the girls a toboggan, putting metal along the runners, and it could really go. They were always a hit with the other kids when they'd show up pulling their toboggan so they could take turns riding it.

The lake just outside of Bowbells froze in the winter, but the wind usually caused the surface to ripple making it too rough for ice skating. Once in a while, it would be smooth enough and those with skates took advantage of it.

The girls knew that Sam had a pair of ice skates and asked him to put them on and skate, but he kept saying, "Nei, I haven't skated for years, and I can't remember how." But they kept pleading until he finally relented. He'd brought the skates all the way from Norway only to store them away in a chest.

Edna ran to get them, and he hung them around his neck as he had so often in Norway where ice skating and skiing were a part of life, and they hurried off to the lake.

Someone had built a fire on the lakeshore, and there were a few people standing around it to get warm. There were several people already skating, and Sam tried to talk his way out of it, but it was no use. He'd have to get the skates on and get out on the ice. When he finally did, the girls held their breath when he took the first step onto the ice, but then all his inhibitions fell away as he glided to the center of the ice to skate for his daughters, gliding and twirling, then on one foot in a figure eight that led into a spin. He was even more graceful than when he and Dora danced.

The girls stood, their hands cupping their cheeks in excitement as they watched. That was their dad! But as far as any one knew, he never skated again.

The school bus, which consisted of an old truck with benches in the bed, when the weather was good to a sled pulled behind a team of horses when snow was too deep for the truck or the ice was too dangerous.

It was a day in May when they'd had a freak snowstorm over the weekend that left snow piled to just under the windows of the house. Sam and Dora didn't think there was much sense in trying to get to the school sled when school was being let out for summer vacation that week anyway, but the girls thought differently and Edna insisted, "We're practicing for the spring concert. We have to go, the concert is Friday night." Both Luella and Alice were like echoes saying, "We have to go."

At last, Dora agreed, and they started off. They had to walk right over a three-foot fence on the way, but then they saw the sled waiting by the side of the road as Sarah and Johnny Johnson waved. Johnny hollered, "Come on, hurry up!"

When they kicked the snow from their feet before climbing in, Mr. Johnson said, "We'd just about given you up."

Luella smiled, "Sorry, Mom couldn't make up her mind if we should go or not."

Once Mr. Johnson had them all bundled in, he said, "Well, I wasn't exactly sure if we should go either. The snow's mighty deep in places. But these two talked me into it."

On the way to the school in town, the horses sank deep in the snow and struggled to keep going and then once they reached the school, they learned that theirs was the only bus to arrive, so they turned around and following their tracks back, they went home.

In a few days, the snow was nearly gone, the weather had warmed, and the concert went on, on schedule.

Dalymare's farm had a manure carrier in the pig barn that ran on a rail overhead, taking the manure from the barn to a pit outside. Dora was putting ground corn in the pigs troughs, a job Carl usually did, when suddenly and accidentally, she tripped the lever dumping the manure right over her. All she could do was run to the well and fortunately, it hadn't hit her face. Margaret came running and dumped pail after pail of water over her. How awful, but Dora was glad it hadn't been Carl, or she knew he would be long gone.

All Margaret could say was "Mom, you smell something fierce!"

They moved into the house in town when it was only partly finished. Mr. Dalymare had given Sam and Dora some nice furniture as part payment for their work on the farm, and Sam had painted the girls' chests of drawers, each in a different color, and carried them upstairs to their rooms. Luella had kept the secret and shared in the surprise with her sisters. After all, she didn't know what color they would be.

Beauty and Wilson had been taken to Ole and Ella's when Sam and Dora moved from the farm, but shortly after moving into the house by the ballpark, Ole came to say that the team had gotten into a barrel of grain and foundered themselves. He said, "Ya . . . they're in a bad way. You better come along and see to them."

Wilson died, and Beauty who had gone blind was brought to Bowbells so they could care for her. Dora was beside herself with grief. Her beautiful Beauty, blind and sick.

* * *

The girls often stopped to visit their grandmother on the way home from school, and one day, Mary asked, "Would you girls like to pick dandelions for Mrs. Larabee? She asked me to ask you."

"You mean dandelion greens?" Edna wrinkled her nose. "Mom cooked them once, but we didn't care much about them, and Dad said it was like eating grass, so she never cooked them again."

"Nei. She wants you to pick just the dandelion heads, just the flower part. She makes wine from them."

"Oh," said Luella. "I suppose we could. How many does she want?"

"She said she will pay you 1¢ for every quart you bring her."

Alice's eyes lit up. "Let me help."

Mary went to a shelf and brought three quart-size jars and gave one to each of them. "Here you are, and you can start in my yard. I have a few of those pesky flowers I'd like to get rid of."

When the jars were full, they took them to Mrs. Larabee who took one look and said, "Oh my, no. The jars have to be packed." And she dumped all three jars into one and, packing them down with her fingers, said, "See? Like this." And dumped the jar full of dandelion flowers into a bowl and handed the jars back to them. Going to a cupboard, she brought a penny and handed it to Luella.

All in all, by the time they'd picked enough for a batch of wine, they had earned 10¢ between them.

This was well into the years of prohibition, which had little or no effect on most anyone in the family, but it was then that one of the aunts decided to make a batch of home brew in a tub on the porch. It was almost ready to bottle when someone came by to say that the feds were in the vicinity, and since no one was at home except one of the older children, he got scared and poured the beer into the pig's trough. Needless to say, there was an angry mother and a bunch of drunken pigs and the feds never showed up.

* * *

It was the spring of 1928, and Sam had ordered several gallons of white house paint, and when it arrived, the family went to work painting the house. It would then be finished and ready to be insured.

Clara Olsen stopped by in the afternoon on her way to Pederson's store to admire the house and ask, "What color will you paint the trim?"

Dora studied the trim around a window for a moment and said, "Just white for now."

"Oh, that always looks nice. Kind of clean like." And she went on her way.

One or the other of the girls would often spend the night with their grandmother and Mary always enjoyed the company even though Sam and Dora lived only a short block away.

This particular night, it was Edna's turn. The two had sat in the swing in the yard until it was dark enough for the street lamps to come on, the signal that it was time for Mary to light the lamp and make cocoa before going to bed.

Sometime during the night, Mary woke up. Sitting up in the bed, she pulled the lace curtain that hung over the window to one side and looked out to see a red glow from somewhere down the street. She knew it was fire!

Alarmed, Mary nudged Edna and called, "Edna, Edna, wake up!" By this time, she was out of bed and halfway dressed.

Down the street, the family as well as Delmar Erickson, the hired man had been sound asleep when smoke drifted beneath Sam and Dora's bedroom door, waking Dora. She yelled, "Sam! Sam! Fire!" And she bounded out of bed with Sam right beside her as they reached the door.

He yelled, "Stand back!" as he opened the door, and a rush of intense heat hit them. Flames rushed up the walls about them as they shouted at the children asleep upstairs. As Sam started up to get them, Margaret and Luella came dragging a screaming Alice down the stairs. He started to push them out the back door when Margaret suddenly stopped in her tracks. "Delmar" and she dashed back up the stairs calling his name until he appeared and followed her back down and out the door.

No one could convince Dora that Edna was not still in the burning house as she fought to get back in to save her. It wasn't until Edna and her grandmother came running into the yard that she believed that Edna was safe.

They had escaped with only their nightclothes and a rocking chair with a faded and worn housedress and a pair of torn and patched bib overalls hanging over the back.

Someone had run for the fire truck only to find it out of water, so all they could do was watch it burn and cry.

As they stood helplessly watching it burn, someone asked, "Do you have insurance?"

Sam answered with tears running down his face, "Not a bit!"

Someone else asked, "How did it happen?"

Right then, Sam had no idea how it had happened, and right then, he didn't care. It had happened, and the important thing was that his family was safe as they huddled there together.

Sam had grabbed the old bib overalls from the back of the chair and pulled them on over the long underwear he'd slept in. They were all barefooted, and Dora and the girls were still in their long nightgowns now smudged in black soot from the fire.

Luella and Alice were crying and huddled against Margaret when Edna came, and Luella pulled her close and said as if it were the only thing that mattered. "Our dressers are burning up!"

The fire still raged as Mrs. Berget came running to rush the three younger girls toward her house next door calling over her shoulder. "Dora, I'm taking the girls to my house." And Dora nodded.

The girls rushed to the window facing their burning house, but Mrs. Berget pulled them away saying, "You mustn't get so close to the window. It might break from the heat."

Luella was still worrying about the dressers when Mrs. Berget said, "It's all right, your dad will build you new ones. You're all safe. That's all that matters."

Soon the reason for the fire was known when Delmar admitted his negligence of coming home drunk and the belief that he'd left a cigarette burning in his car when he went into the house. It had already been determined that the fire had started there in his automobile, and though he was held accountable by everyone else in town, Sam and Dora knew it had been an accident. He would never have done such a thing intentionally drunk or sober.

The family was put to bed at Mary's for the rest of the night, but no one slept.

The morning found Sam and Dora sifting through the charred debris in the basement where all that remained had fallen, searching for the only money they had in the world. All they found was a glob of melted coins. Any paper money was gone forever.

When Anton and Annie and Ole and Ella learned of the fire, they came with bedding and whatever they could spare. Anton asked Sam, "Syver, why didn't you get insurance?"

Sam who was getting tired of hearing the same question said, "You can't get insurance on a place until it's finished, and we just finished painting yesterday. As a matter of fact, the wet oil paint was probably the biggest reason for the fire."

"Ya, it's too bad." And he turned to Annie. "Did you bring them shoes? They should fit Syver."

Annie brought them from the car. "Here, try these on. He never wears 'em."

They were shiny black patent leather with a buckle, but they were a good fit.

It became a sort of joke because Sam wore them with the patched bib overalls and a faded red plaid shirt with the sleeves torn off at the elbows and people would ask. "You on your way to a dance, Sam?" It provided some laughter in a time of tragedy, and Sam enjoyed the humor as much as anyone, clowning it up as he tipped his hat and danced about though his heart was breaking.

Soon after the fire friends and neighbors brought household goods and clothing, hoping to fit someone in the family. It was the shoes that were given them that were the biggest problem.

Luella's were so tight they caused her to develop bunions though she never once complained, or at least not to her folks. Alice's were worn so badly on one side of the sole that she walked at a slant, and Margaret's were too big. Dora was given a pair of her mother's that almost fit, and of course, Sam had the black patent leather shoes.

Edna was the only one to have her own shoes, but even she had only the clothes, she had on when she went to her grandmother's, everything else that was hers burned in the fire.

Margaret was going on sixteen and about to be married to her beau, Ben Skredsvig, but the wedding was postponed because she was needed to help after the fire.

Luella, twelve; Edna, ten; and Alice, seven helped as well to clean up the mess from the fire before Sam moved another shell of a house he'd gotten for $300 on to the foundation of the house that had burned. It didn't fit exactly, but he improvised and made it work.

Within a month's time while still working out for others to earn enough to sustain them, he had the house closed in and finished enough to move in. They would live in two rooms while he finished the rest. That man, he could do the impossible but he was not alone, he had a wife who could do the same.

In the meantime, Dora had taken a job of cleaning house for Mrs. Wiper, the banker's wife, and during that time, they all lived with Mary in her tiny house.

Once the family moved into their house, Margaret and Ben were married and went to live on the farm he owned not too far from his mother's in the hills, and they started the first year of many as husband and wife.

* * *

Mary's days were now spent with her knitting as she listened to the sounds of the small yellow canary that Sam had gotten for her. She looked up to watch as it flitted about the cage before landing on its perch where it seemed to look at her and twitter its sweet song.

Her vegetable and flower garden were her pride and joy in the summer, and her houseplants during the winter when it was cold.

Mary had been thinking a lot about Denmark lately, and she remembered the news they'd gotten about the evacuation of German troops from her beautiful *Abenraa*. She remembered the way Lana had described it.

> How wonderful it was to watch as Germany evacuated their army. Watching their stiff-legged march as they marched to the waiting trucks and then it was over. They were gone, and though I'd never known a time when they weren't here, the relief was blessed. A hush seemed to fall over the city, if but for a moment.

Mary sat reminiscing when a tap sounded on the door, and Dora burst in. "My, it's cold out there!" she said. "I have a letter for you from Denmark." As she took off her scarf and unbuttoned her coat, she handed the letter to her mother.

"Well, what do you know, I was just thinking about home. Sit down, and I'll read it to you."

My dear Mary,

I couldn't wait to tell you of your captain's visit. You have asked about him several times.

He is old and not very well and wanted to know about you and John and the children. He was saddened to hear about John's death.

I asked him about Dora, his cook, and he was noticeably saddened at what he told me.

It seems she was arrested and taken to the German compound. The captain said they had told him that Dora had taken several valuable paintings and some valuable dog statuettes from the home where she worked before going to work for the captain.

The paintings were indeed found hidden in the captain's kitchen, but the dog statuettes were never found. He did say that it had been the people who she had worked for who asked her to take the paintings and statuettes to keep the Germans from taking them but she never told.

The captain said he had tried to have Dora released but was nearly accused of being a party to the theft himself.

Dora was held for nearly six years, and I am sure it will be no surprise to you to know where. She was held as head cook in the officer's kitchen until Denmark regained sovereignty and the Germans left.

Dora is back in the captain's kitchen, but he said she is not the same Dora.

Your sister, Lana

When Mary finished reading, she laid the letter in her lap, and with a twinkle in her eye, she said, "Well, what do you know about that? After all these years, and those dogs have been in my china cabinet."

"Ma? Do you mean," as she pointed toward the pair of dog statuettes behind the glass of the cabinet. "That they are the ones that Aunt Lana is talking about?"

"Yes, they must be . . ." and Mary went to the cabinet, and taking them out, she handed them to Dora. "There. How does it feel to be holding something so famous?"

"I don't want to, I might drop them." And she put them back inside the cabinet.

"They are no different now than they were before we knew their value. Come on, let's have a cup of coffee and a donut. I made a batch this morning."

As they sat at the table, one or the other would titter and say, "Isn't that something?" Or "Can you imagine? All this time, we never knew," always referring of course to the dog statuettes.

"Just wait until Mary Inga and Ella hear about it. Can you imagine what Mary Inga will say?"

"Ya, now she will want them. She has never liked them, you know. She used to tease me for wrapping them so carefully when I'd put them in the 'American Trunk' when we'd move somewhere. Of course, I was careful of them because they were some of the few things I was able to bring from the old country and because Dora, the captain's cook, had given them to me as a wedding gift."

All this talk about the old country made Dora think about another aunt. "Ma, what about Auntie in Flaxton? I can remember when she and her children came and stayed with us for a while but where was her husband?"

"Ufda! That was sad. It seems that Sophus Ewald, her husband, had come to America a short while before and then sent for Anna and the children. They had five children. Let me see if I can remember their names. There is Carl, Marie, Agnus, Annie, and Alvina, and Anna was expecting their sixth. But when Anna came, Sophus didn't meet her, and she didn't know what to do, so she sent a telegram to us for help. We sent her the money and told her how to get to Bowbells. When she came, she had so many trunks and parcels that we could barely pay the shipping charge. Anyway, she stayed with us just a short time and then moved into Bowbells where the baby was born but the baby died shortly after it was born. I believe her name was Elsie."

"But what about her husband?" Dora asked impatiently.

"Anna learned that he returned to Denmark or Germany soon after he sent for her to come to America, leaving her stranded and penniless in Philadelphia where she arrived. I don't know if she ever learned the full story, but it was no surprise to me that he would do such a thing."

"Oh why, was he always kind of a skunk?"

"You might say that." And Mary left it at that.

"Why do we always call her Auntie in Flaxton? I know she lives there, but it's like it's kind of a title."

"Oh, I don't know. I guess it's because she married Ole Rose after she divorced Sophus, and they live in Flaxton. I don't know of any other reason. Why all this interest in Tanta Anna?"

"Just curious! I've always wondered and never thought to ask before. I remember when John and Alma were born, and we went to see them, but I haven't seen Auntie in Flaxton for quite a while. Oh yes, and what about Lauritz Adamson. Who is he? I mean, I know who he is, but how does he fit into the family?"

"Oh my, you are curious today," Mary said as she lifted the lid of the big iron cook stove and added a few chunks of coal, and opening the draft, she slid the coffee pot to the hottest spot. "There, the coffee will be hot in a minute, and we'll have another cup." Settling back in her chair, she said. "Now about Lauritz. He is your Pa's nephew. You remember hearing about Pa and his brother Per being given away when their baby sister was born and their mother died, or no maybe you don't . . . anyway, Lauritz is that baby sister's son. I guess she never married and no one really knows what became of her or how her son happened to end up coming and settling here so close to his uncle, your pa. I expect that the uncle in Iowa knows more about it. Per suggested that he did. Now how about a cup of coffee?" And she rose to pour the coffee and set on a plate of bread and a jar of her chokecherry jelly and pushed the plate with the remaining two donuts over to Dora.

"He is quite a handsome man, but he doesn't talk much. I can only remember of seeing him a few times, and then only when he came to visit you before Pa died. Is it true that he was a German sympathizer during the war?"

"Goodness, I hope not. Your brother Mil and my brothers were in that awful war and enough about Lauritz." Changing the subject, she said, "I have a few pair of socks for Sam. They were Pa's, and some have been darned, but they've still got some wear in them." Mary took them from a drawer and handed them to Dora.

"Sam will be glad to have them, thank you, Ma. I better be getting home. I still can hardly believe how valuable those dog statuettes are. I guess a person never knows."

Dora was a good seamstress and mourned the loss of her sewing machine that had burned in the fire. She needed it now especially when they all needed new clothing so badly. It was good they had gotten clothes from friends and neighbors, but so many were ill fitting or nearly worn out, and it was hard for the girls to show up in school with one of their classmates' hand-me-downs. And Sam, my goodness, he looked like a ragamuffin. He would need some new store-bought overalls and shoes. Oh my, yes, and shoes! She would make him a new shirt or two.

Mrs. Berget came one day with the news that she had just purchased a brand new electric-model sewing machine and asked, "Dora, do you have any need of a good treadle sewing machine? I just got a new one. I mean to say, I got a new electric model, but my treadle machine works just fine."

"Well, yes, I could certainly use it. How much do you want for it?"

"Oh my, no, you can have it."

"Are you sure?"

"Yes! Maybe Sam can come to get it this evening. I really want it out of my way, and Simon isn't feeling very good."

And so it was that Dora had a sewing machine. Now all she needed was yard goods and a few spools of thread.

When the machine was brought home, Dora found needles and several spools of thread and a pair of scissors, a cloth measuring tape, and a thimble in the drawers. She said to Sam, "My goodness, you don't realize how many things you need until you don't have them. Isn't this nice? Mrs. Berget thought of just about everything."

All he said was "ya! Now you can sew." Dora knew how discouraged he felt, how much he wanted to provide the things they needed, but she knew too that everything would look better in the morning as he always said.

Since it was summer, she could wait to think about making coats, but the girls needed dresses and Sam, shirts.

Two of the dresses they were given were large with full-gathered skirts and the fabric was nice, one pink with little white flowers and the other was blue with a white and green design. Another was darker blue and had a more straight skirt but was quite long, and the bodice had a large sailor type collar and long full sleeves.

When the dresses were finished, Luella's was the darker blue with a smaller version of the white sailor collar, a pleated skirt, and white buttons.

Edna's was the blue with the white and green design and a white scalloped collar edged in blue with a wide sash that tied in the back over a gathered skirt and white buttons down the front of the bodice.

Alice's dress was the pink with the little white flowers and a round collar with a white inset down the front of the bodice and pink buttons. It too had a wide sash over a gathered skirt.

They were all quite beautiful and the envy of many of their school friends.

Dora was asked to sew for some of the women in town, and she did occasionally, but she neither had the time nor the inclination. It was quite enough to keep her family clothed.

Enough yard goods were purchased to make Sam two shirts and a pair of overalls and a pair of shoes was bought. Dora cut down one of her mother's dresses for herself, and in the meantime, whenever there was a spare moment, she would pick up her knitting to finish a sock, and this was only the beginning.

When Margaret was expecting her first baby, she came one day with news. "Mom, have you ever heard of a lady by the name of Maude Barr? She lives not far from Ben and me. Anyway, she is a midwife and will come when I need her."

"Won't you want Doc Hilts?"

"Well, yes, but what if he doesn't get there in time, and Mrs. Barr lives so close."

"I don't know Maude Barr," said Dora, "but I've heard she's delivered a lot of babies. That's good that she'll be so close. I could bring Grandma if we knew when—" and Dora laughed and said, "But we don't."

"I wish Grandma could come, but I know she can't. Does she ever deliver babies anymore?"

"It's been quite a while now, but did you know that she has delivered more than fifty babies?" I remember one of the first. I was only little because Ella was just a baby, but I remember how worried Pa was. He hadn't been home when a man came flying into the yard with his team and buckboard, and after he talked to Ma for a minute, she ran into the house and got Ella and climbed up beside the man and away they went. I guess she'd told Mary Inga that she was going to deliver a baby, but she didn't know where or who the man was. All I remember is that she was gone a long time before the man brought her and Ella home."

Dora had been seated at the sewing machine the whole time she talked and then lifted a small flannel gown from the machine and after breaking the thread, she turned and handed it to Margaret. "Here . . . this is for my first grandchild. There are a few other things I've made laying on that chair." As she pointed to a small stack of receiving blankets and a little crocheted sweater.

"Oh, Mom, thank you. This is a big help. Now I'd better get for home." At the door, she stopped and turned. "Did you say fifty babies?"

"Yup!"

"Oh my goodness . . ." And Margaret left.

Margaret and Ben's baby, a little girl they named Doris Kathryn, came in the coldest part of winter just before the new year of 1929. It was December 13, 1928.

* * *

Old Pete Anderson, as the folks in town called him, had been a friend of John and Mary for many years, and so it was only natural that he should remain Mary's friend after John died. He would come by at seven thirty three evenings a week and leave exactly at nine. He would always bring either a candy bar or something sweet to go with their coffee. He and Mary and whichever of the grandchildren that was staying that night would play a game of rummy, or he would tell them some outlandish tale or bring his guitar or violin and play for them, tapping his toe as he played. He was a brilliant and talented man as well as eccentric. His carvings were very inventive, like the ferris wheel that stood some two feet high with seats that swung and carved people riding in them. The ferris wheel turned and was powered by a wind-up clock and a music box that played carousel music.

Pete Anderson had a 1914 Model-T touring car that looked like new. Each winter, he removed the wheels and jacked the car up in the garage and left it until just before Memorial Day when he would get it ready to take Mary and sometimes one or all of the girls to the cemetery to put flowers on John's grave as well as others'. The car was used but a few times a year and never on trips over twenty miles.

*   *   *

Sam was still juggling his time between carpentry jobs and the farm, and in 1930, the family moved back out to the farm. Margaret and Ben had had their second baby, a little boy they named Alfred Leroy born May 24, and Edna had graduated from the eighth grade.

The Depression had started, and the news of people leaping from windows as a result of losing everything—their money and all that they owned—trickled down over the wires from New York and other big cities, but it hadn't really affected the farmers in the Dakotas as yet. But that year was the beginning of what would become known as the dust bowl or the dirty thirties.

All the beautiful horses that Sam and Dora owned had now been replaced with two nags. Slim, who was tall and so sway backed they hardly needed a saddle to ride him, and Dolly, who was not much better. This team wandered off and got into a neighbors barn and ate some treated grain. When the neighbor came to tell Sam, it was Luella and Edna who rode along with him and walked the horses home. It took a long time because the horse's legs were so swollen, a consequence of eating the treated grain, and had they not walked, they would have died right then and there. All the way home, the horses seemed to take turns stopping and it took either Luella or Edna to pull and the other to push and switch its backside to get them going again. It was a long way home. Later, one of those horses died, and the other was retired, and they got another, a much better team but none of them could measure up to Beauty and Wilson or the other teams from years past.

Being the baby for the last ten years, Alice was not exactly thrilled with the knowledge that her mother was expecting a baby. However, the possibility of the baby being a boy did create a glimmer of excitement. But if it should be another girl, it would mean losing her status as the youngest and have to take her place in the order of things. In so doing, change to being one of the big kids or rather an addition to the 'little kids' as Luella and Edna had always been called. It had always been, Margaret as 'Toots,' and the 'little kids,' who were Luella as 'Sissy' and Edna as 'Moony' and now Alice as 'Babe,' as she'd always been known.

The first part of March, Sam and Dora went back to Bowbells to be near Doc Hilts for the birth of their fifth child, and on the afternoon of the sixteenth, Dora went into labor, but it was soon learned that something was terribly wrong. The baby was not only breech, turned the wrong way in her mother's womb, but also in a wrong position with her little legs resting on her abdomen and there was no way of turning her. Once she was finally born on the morning of March seventeenth after much trauma to both mother and baby, it was discovered that some of the baby's organs were protruding from her small body. It was Mrs. Berget who was helping Doc Hilts who gently poked them back inside. The tops of her legs as well as her abdomen were raw when they straightened her body, and she would require a great deal of care. Doc Hilts told Sam, "She will most likely not be able to have children."

But in later years, she proved him wrong! They named her Ethel Dorothy.

That summer, the banker persuaded Sam to run some seventy-five head of cattle on his place and the land around the lake that Sam rented. They were cattle the bank had foreclosed on, and he had nowhere to keep them.

Luella and Edna spent most of their time herding these cattle, and while they kept track of the cattle, they searched for Indian arrowheads. They uncovered grass-covered mounds and found stone hammers and other implements chiseled from stone. Those were fun times, but the clouds of despair were gathering on the horizon.

Wild flowers on the North Dakota Plains were phenomenal—bright, delicate crocus, in purple and blue, red bells and bluebells, pink roses and bright orange tiger lily, and the wonderful fragrance of the buffalo brush. And of course, the fields of bright blue flax.

There were berries too—June berries, wild strawberries, chokecherries and occasionally vines of wild grape. But with the drought, even though it was early in the dirty thirties, these delicacies became increasingly harder to find, and the flowers withered and died before they had a chance to bloom. No one missed these things more than Sam and Dora and the girls.

The banker's herd grew, and he persuaded Sam to buy fifty of them, mostly young stock, but there were now too many for just Luella and Edna to herd, so Sam made a deal with Maynard Goodyjohn. He presented the idea of a place for he and his wife whom he called Honey, and their little girl called Bunny to live, in exchange for Maynard to herd the cattle. The deal was struck, and Sam proceeded to divide their house right down the middle. It proved to be less than a comfortable situation for either family and especially after Maynard's wife had their baby, a boy they named Sonny.

Maynard made other living arrangements, and the Berg's house was put back to as normal as was possible. All except the one room that set it apart from any other house, the vestibule.

It was then that the banker took his share of the cattle for slaughter and Luella and Edna were back to herding. Sam hired Mugs Gleave to help. The Gleave family lived just north of the school land that Sam rented surrounding the small lake where the cattle were watered and pastured.

There were no crops to speak of by this time in '32 and the wind seemed to blow constantly. Dust blew into and onto everything, and on washday, it seemed almost futile to hang clothes on the line. Each time they hoped against hope that the wind would quiet until the clothes were dry, but it rarely happened. Lines were strung beneath the rafters of the porch roof, but it was of little help. The wind blew the dust in beneath the porch roof and onto the clothes. And when Dora strung a short line just for underwear, so they wouldn't feel so gritty against the skin, in the smoke house, they all ended up smelling like ham or smoked sausage, so from then on, they found a place to dry in the house.

It was almost a relief when winter came, looking forward to the clean white snow though the snow was dry with little moisture to feed the parched ground.

Ben and Margaret were farming and having a hard go of it, as was everyone else, and it was also when their third baby came along. Lyle Bernard was his name, and it was a particularly stormy day that December 28. It was a good thing that Maude Barr lived close by because Doc Hilts would never have made it in time, if at all.

The Depression was heightening its effects on the farming communities, devastatingly linking it with the drought. The fields were not yielding enough grain to feed the stock or to grind into flour for bread for the farmer's tables, so they were left to the mercy of the government.

Rationing of flour at the mills meant storing it for longer times, and when Dora went to get their allotment, she found weevils in the flour when she got home. There was nothing to do but sift it over and over again and hope that she'd gotten them all.

Sam was working at carpentry most of the time now, but money was tight so wages were low. He often worked for little or nothing, just to help someone who needed help. But when the banker hired him to craft and install the beautiful and intricate moldings, he was to be paid 25¢ an hour, and it was what Sam expected since the banker was not among those without means, but when all was said and done, he was paid just 12 ½¢ and never received the rest. It was always the same old line. "Sam, you know me, I'll make it good with you." And Sam fell for it every time because he believed in people. Dora, however, exploded every time this happened because for one reason, she saw through the banker, and for another, she didn't like her Sam to be taken advantage of, and for yet another reason: they needed the money.

But Sam would tell her, "Now, Dory, don't we always have enough? I know things could be better but we have enough for now. You'll see, One of these days, things will be better, and then you'll look back and ask yourself why you worried."

"I know, I suppose you're right," she'd say. But for now, it was hard to be so positive.

The grass-covered hills where they herded the cattle were brown from lack of rain, and even the lake land. Only close to the water of the lake was the grass still green, but the lake itself was growing smaller and smaller, and the herd was growing larger with new calves.

Sam was able to sell a few head of cattle now and then, often in trade for hay, but as time went on, it was growing harder and harder to feed the ones they had. Hay was no longer plentiful enough for winter, and with snow so often on the ground or the few blades of grass frozen, it was hard. The only thing that carried them through was the wheat left in the granary on the farm. Wheat that was really unfit for flour or anything else, but it was all they had. What hay remaining in the barn's loft would feed the livestock for a time, but not for long.

The cattle had to be herded to the lake to drink every day, and when it was really cold, Luella and Edna would watch one another for signs of frostbite on their faces. And if white spots should appear, they'd rub their faces with snow until the skin turned pink. They'd seen people who'd had frostbite where the skin turned black, sometimes even losing toes or ears. Luella had once seen a man with only part of a nose from frostbite so they were very careful.

They got their first radio with its many batteries when Luella and Edna raised turkeys and sold them. They occasionally got a program from as far away as Moose Jaw, Canada, or El Paso, Texas, though at times all they heard was static. They looked forward to westerns like Tom Mix and the Lone Ranger and the B Bar B Boys, they laughed with Burns and Allen, Amos 'n' Andy and Jack Benny and sat on the edge of their seats through Sherlock Holms and the Shadow Knows and tapped their toes to the tunes on National Barn Dance and the Grand Ole Opry, Guy Lombardo, and Al Jolson.

* * *

Dora was now expecting her and Sam's sixth child sometime in early November as near as she could figure. Sam would be almost fifty years old, and Dora, thirty-eight. Sometimes it seemed they had lived a lifetime together counting their many blessings, putting any bad times behind them, and now another blessing? They could have easily thought, *As if the drought and the depression were not enough, that now there would be yet another mouth to feed.* But they didn't, or at least they never voiced it.

Winter was fast approaching when Sam took Dora, Alice and Ethel back into town until after the baby was born. Luella and Edna would stay on the farm to do chores and to watch so no one stole gas or any of the little feed they had left. People were hard pressed and would sometimes do what they might think the unthinkable in better times.

Maynard Goodyjohn and Mugs Gleave drove the herd to the lake for water and helped where they could, but Sam hired Mugs to stay with the girls to help with the chores and to cut ice for the water barrel at the house, but he was often sick with tonsillitis.

Sam came when he could but it was up to him to work enough for others to support the family.

Dora had been having pains throughout the day, and by nightfall, she knew her time was near.

Sam asked, "Should I get Ma to stay with you while I go after Doc Hilts?"

"No, Ma hasn't been feeling a bit good. Alice is here if I need anything, but you'd better get going."

It was only a short time after Doc Hilts got there that he came from the bedroom with a grin on his face and announced, "It's another girl!"

Sam grinned from ear to ear as he headed for the bedroom to see Dora, but Alice sat on a chair with her elbows on her knees and her head in her hands and said, "Oh no! Not again."

They had already decided on the name of Mary after both of their mothers, and just in case the baby was a boy, he would have been named Stanley Duane. *Just in case, mind you.* The same boy's name picked out from the time Margaret was born but never used.

And so it was, Mary Delores Berg. Born on November 10, 1933.

Sam went out to the farm to tell the girls of their new sister's arrival and to bring coal and food supplies that Dora was sure they must need.

Edna asked, "When will you be coming back to the farm so we can see the baby Mary?"

"I'm not sure yet, but Doc Hilts thinks momma should stay in town for a while longer."

The girls looked scared and said in unison, "Is Mom sick?"

"Nei! She just needs to gain her strength back. Nothing to worry about, but she's worried about you girls being by yourselves for Christmas."

Luella protested, "We'll be fine. Tell Mom not to worry."

And Edna, trying to sound as brave, said, "Yes, we'll be fine."

Dora was not well after Mary was born, so they would stay in town for a while longer. It would mean not being with Luella and Edna for Christmas, but with Alice's help she would bake their favorite cookies and make fudge and penuche. She would send a bowl of mashed potatoes so the girls could bake lefsa on top of the cook stove and a ham to bake in the oven.

It was nearing Christmas, and the girls were trying to decide what to make everyone for Christmas. They had a saw, hammer, and nails and some scraps of lumber. What more could they want?

Luella would build a medicine cabinet for their folks and Edna a scooter for Ethel, which she would share with Mary when she was bigger. Luella pondered, *What should we make for Alice? Oh let's see . . . what can we make for her?*

"I know, a jewelry box." Edna looked pleased with herself for thinking of it, but Luella said, "Ya, but she hasn't got any jewelry."

"Well, than what about a hankie box? She has a hankie."

Luella relented and said, "Oh all right. A hankie box."

They were done with the Christmas projects when Luella decided she needed to paint the medicine cabinet. She found a can of paint and a brush and went to work. It looked pretty good, but a week later, the paint was just as tacky as it was the day after it was painted, and it never got any better. They set it by the stove, out on the porch, tried rubbing it, but nothing helped.

A few days before Christmas, they were surprised and happy when Sam brought Alice to spend Christmas vacation with them. They were delighted at the sight of cookies and candy, but when Alice pointed out the bowl of mashed potatoes for lefsa, they almost cried; they were so happy.

Edna took the sticky medicine cabinet and scooter out to the back seat of the car while

Sam went to the barn to check on some of the animals and hurried to bring in more kindling and filled the coal shuttle before he had to go, but he took time to have a cup of coffee and hear the news since he'd been out last.

Edna looked at Luella and grinned. "Tell Dad about the gas!"

Luella knew what she was talking about, but didn't let on so Edna told it herself.

"Some guy came and said he needed some gas. He said he knew we had some, and it sounded like he wasn't going to take no for an answer, so Lu told him to wait and she'd get him some. Well, anyway, she went around to the back of the house where she'd set the pee pot. We hadn't dumped it yet, and she poured it in a gallon jar and brought it to him. She'd added some water to fill it up. It looked just like gas. Anyway, he took it and left."

By the time she'd gotten to the end of the story, Sam was in tears from laughing so hard.

Then he got serious, "Next time, if anybody comes like that, don't open the door. Make him think no one is home. I'm sure sorry that you girls have to be here alone."

But Luella said, "It's okay, Dad, we'll be fine. After all, we're not little kids."

After Sam left, Lu said, "See? That's why I didn't want to tell him. Now he'll worry about us."

Alice said, "He already does worry, but at least he laughed at the way you handled it." Then she turned toward the box of things they'd brought, and they all took a cookie.

The next morning, they made lefsa. Luella added the flour to the mashed potatoes. Two cups for every six cups of potato that was already mixed with lard and cream. Stirring in the flour, she took a ball of dough, and laying it on the covered and floured board, she rolled it this way and that until it was thin and as round as she could get it. But they all laughed as they named the shapes as looking like a dog or a cow or something funny and few were round as they should be. Then she wound it onto the lefsa stick, and then unwound it onto the top of the hot cook stove.

Edna then took the stick from Luella and watched until the top was bubbled, lifting an edge every so often to see if it was done, and then turning it over with the stick, she baked the other side before lifting it from the stove to put between two folded pieces of clean old sheet blanket to keep it soft.

They took turns at rolling and turning, with Alice filling in with the turning and adding coal to the fire.

By the time they were through, their mouths were watering, and they each took the most ragged lefsa they could find at the bottom of the pile and spread it with butter and ate it. They would keep the best ones for Christmas dinner.

On Christmas Eve morning, Alice asked which of them wanted their hair curled first. She had brought the curling iron along so they could all be curled and beautiful for Christmas. Edna was first as Alice lit the lantern and laid the curling part of the iron over the flame and waited for it to get hot. When she was finished, Edna had a head full of dark curls. Lu was next but halfway through, she dozed off and nearly fell off the chair, but when Alice was finished, she too had curls.

Alice decided she would curl her own hair, and that is what she did.

Christmas was always celebrated on Christmas Eve as most Scandinavians did. The ham their mother had sent was put in the oven in the late morning, and Lu got everything else ready to cook while Edna and Mugs went to do chores. Mugs would first eat with them and then go home to his family for the evening.

By one o'clock, Alice had the table set. She'd ironed the nicest tablecloth they had and used the best of the dishes and silverware. She had even cut squares of muslin for napkins and stood a candle in a blue jar and tied a red ribbon around it for the center of the table. It was ready for the food. Baked ham, potatoes and gravy, sweet potato, beet pickles, and glorified rice, and of course, the lefsa, cookies, and candy.

The three girls with curly hair and a young man with slicked-down hair ate until they could eat no more and laughed at anything and everything before singing carols around a buck brush tree. Lu and Edna gave Alice the hankie box that she said she loved, and she gave them each a handmade Christmas card. All in all, it was a wonderful Christmas Eve though they missed the presence of the rest of the family.

Christmas morning after Mugs came, they all went out and fed the livestock just a little more than usual and spread a little feed for the birds.

There was a break in the weather just after Christmas when Margaret and Ben and the kids drove into the yard of the farm and piled out. Five-year-old Doris ran up the stairs of the house with three-year-old Alfred, who was always called Bud, right behind her. Before they could knock, the door flew open and Luella scooped Bud up in her arms and grabbed Doris's hand. Alice came from the house and down the stairs to take Margaret's hand while Ben carried little Lyle.

Margaret said as she squeezed Alice's hand, "I didn't expect to see you. When did you come?"

"Dad brought me a few days ago, so Lu and Edna wouldn't be alone on Christmas, and we've been having so much fun."

"Where is Edna?"

"Oh, she and Mugs are doing chores." But just then, Edna came carrying a pail of milk from the barn and greeted her sister.

"Oh good! Now you can have some of the lefsa we made. We made taffy today."

In the house, Lu had put on the coffee, and while they were waiting for it to be done, Edna set the plate of taffy on the, table but try as they might, they couldn't loosen it from the plate.

Even Ben gave up and said, "I think the only way you'll get this taffy loose is to break the plate." And that is exactly what they did, and it all came loose. There was just the matter of brushing a few fragments of pottery from the candy, and in no time, it was all eaten.

It was time for them to go home, and as they got into the car, Margaret who was expecting their fourth child, turned and said, "Tell Dad that we will be in to see them soon. We haven't seen sister Mary yet."

Margaret's face flushed. "It seems funny to think of her as my sister when my baby will be nearly the same age, and Mary will be the aunt, and my baby will be either her niece or nephew."

Just as they started off, Ben leaned out and joked, "Be sure to keep the pee pot full." He'd laughed as Sam had when Edna told them about the man demanding gas.

Sam came to get Alice the next week and said, "We'll be coming back to the farm in a couple of weeks. Your mother looks better. She's got some color back in her cheeks."

"What about me? Will I be staying with Grandma until school is out?" Alice pouted.

"Ya, I don't think the school out here will be open."

It wasn't that she didn't like staying with her grandmother. It was just that when any of them had had to do that in the winter, they always felt like they were missing a lot at home.

* * *

By the end of March, there had still been no rain, and on into April and it was clear that they had no choice but to sell off the cattle or see them die. The government would buy them for a measly twenty to twenty-five dollars a head, but there was nothing else they could do. There was no feed, no hay, and the ground was bare of anything other than buck brush and a few blades of withered grass. Even the buck brush showed no sign of blooming. The one thing they could usually count on was the sweet heavenly smell, and now not even that.

Sam even now said to Dora, "I know the government isn't offering much, but it's better than nothing, and we'll get by." He not only believed that, but he *knew* it to be so.

The day two men came to look at the cattle and worked out the details of price, and getting them to the stockyard in Woburn where they'd be loaded onto railroad cars, Sam brought them in for coffee. This meant coffee and whatever food they had on hand, but at least bread and cheese and maybe some dried beef.

Sitting around the table, Alice looked down at the floor and stiffening, she poked Edna in the side and whispered very seriously. "Look at Ethel!"

Edna, thinking it was funny rather than serious whispered to Dora, suppressing a giggle, she said. "Mom, look at Ethel!"

When she did, Dora's face turned red, and she quickly seized Ethel from off a round loaf of bread she'd taken from a cupboard to sit on, apparently because all the chairs were taken. But as embarrassing as it was for Dora, the humor of it took the edge off an otherwise sad and difficult time.

The amount of twenty dollars a head was agreed on except for Sam and Dora's prize registered short-horn bull that would bring an additional five dollars. Selling that bull for only twenty-five dollars was sickening to say the least.

The day they were to herd the cattle to Woburn neighbors Emlin Kelvic and Clifford Poline drove their cattle to join Sam's herd. Clifford would drive his truck with all the new calves, and Luella, who was suffering with a toothache, would ride with him. She was to sign the paper for Sam that the cattle had been delivered once they got them there.

Edna, Emlin Kelvic, and Tilmar Swanson herded the sum of over one hundred head on horseback the fifteen miles to Woburn. It was late afternoon when they got the last of the herd separated and into the stock pens.

When each head was counted and totaled, Luella signed the order and was given a government check for her dad, but she had Edna double-check the figures before signing and accepting it.

It was about the middle of May when Ben came to get Luella to help with their youngsters when Margaret had the baby, but it wasn't until May 24 that Sylvia Marie was born.

Doris was so happy that she had a sister instead of another brother that she cried and hugged her mother. Lyle, of course, would just as soon there not be either sister or brother. He was only two and didn't care for all the attention that little Sylvia was getting, but he'd get over it, and the two would become very close.

Ben's mother's farm had a large lake, and during these times of hardship for so many, she and her family were able to utilize the lake water to grow enough hay, raise enough garden, and water enough stock to hang on.

Sam and Dora tried to think of some way to make a go of it on the farm but with no crops, and now not even cattle, except the two milk cows, a sow and two piglets left from her litter, and a team of horses—and that was it. The well was showing signs of drying up too. But when the grasshoppers appeared, a swarm darkening the sky before settling to the ground and devouring every blade of withered grass and gnawing the fence posts down in size, the decision was made—they would move back to Bowbells and give up the farm, but right after the move, it began to rain, and Sam decided to go out and put in a crop with what seed he'd saved from the last harvest, now two years before. The crop had been meager, but at least the yield had provided some grain for feed and possibly enough seed for the south forty. There hadn't been even enough for more than one sack of flour that Sam milled himself.

Dora shuddered in remembrance of the flour crawling with weevils that she'd had to get at the mill that year when she ran out of their own.

It rained enough to germinate the seed in the field, and hopes were high among the farmers, but then it stopped raining. And though the clouds gathered and lightning streaked across the sky and thunder rolled, there was no more rain.

* * *

It was now the winter of 1935 when a letter came from Sam's sister in Washington:

> Dear Syver and Dora,
> You have written about the bad crops because of having no rain, and I have wondered if you would consider moving to Washington. There is a lot of work for carpenters, Syver, and especially for those with your skills. And I would like to see you. Maybe you could make a trip out here to see for yourself.
> Your sister, Anna

Neither Sam nor Dora spoke, each in his or her own thoughts, until Sam asked, "What do you think? Should we take a trip out to Washington?"

"Oh, I don't know, you know we can't afford it."

"Ya, I know, but if there is that much work out there . . ."

"Sam, we can't move out there. What about Margaret and Ben and the kids? And Luella is getting married in the spring . . . and Ma . . . we can't leave her!"

"Ya, but we could go to visit, and you've never seen an ocean."

"How can we afford it?"

"I've got a couple of jobs that would give us enough for the trip, and if we drive and pack enough food for the trip, we'd only have to pay for some place to sleep for maybe two or three nights. Let's do it! Should we?"

Dora grinned, showing her excitement. "Yes, let's go! Wait till we tell the kids."

Luella, when she was told about the trip, said, "Oh really? When?"

"In the spring, after the roads are clear in the mountains, I suppose."

Charlie Gleave had proposed to Luella at Christmas, and now she said, "Charlie wants to get married in the spring, but I want to go with you to Washington."

"You could both go, but I'm not sure that we'd all fit in the car."

"No mom, I know we can't, but maybe Charlie will let us postpone the wedding until we get back."

As for Edna and Alice, they could hardly wait for the time to come when the trip would begin. They could hardly wait to see the Pacific Ocean and the mountains, and Alice was already planning what they should wear.

Sam and Dora went to Ben and Margaret's to tell them about the upcoming trip, saying, "We wish you could come along."

"I know." Margaret smiled. "But I know you'll have a good time. When will you go? I hope you wait till it warms up. This winter has been fierce. Oh, and I haven't told you yet, we're having another baby the end of August or early September.

Ben just grinned and said, "We'll take a trip one of these days."

When Luella came with the news that she and Charlie were getting married in April, but that Charlie had said she could go on the trip if they didn't leave until June, everyone cheered.

Luella and Charlie would be married in the Gleave's Parlor, and Edna and Charlie's brother John would stand up for them.

The day of the wedding in April, it hailed so hard it sounded as if it was nearly coming through the roof.

Luella and Charlie went to live on Sam and Dora's farm in the Hills since Sam had turned it back to the bank when they decided to quit farming, and Charlie was able to just take over the payments. Later, he bought another section that was going for taxes.

The day they left for Washington, Edna remembered her camera at the last minute and ran to get it from the house. It was the small Kodak she'd gotten from the Kodak Co. in 1930. Everyone born in 1918 had received one.

Sam had not gotten the license for the car from Bismarck though it had been sent for some time past, and instead of waiting longer, they decided to go through Bismarck to get it though it took them out of the way.

That night, they pulled in beside a group of small cabins in Mandan, a short way west of Bismarck, and unloaded the bedding from the back seat after they'd all climbed out. Luella,

Edna, and Alice had sat on the folded bedding, lying across the back seat to make more room in the trunk for the family's food and cooking utensils and clothing. A bag of coal lay on the floorboards in the back seat where one of the girls would rest her feet and a small bundle of kindling and a box of car tools found a place in the trunk.

Dora and the girls gathered what they'd need for the night from the car while Sam paid for a night's stay in one of the cabins. The mosquitoes were thick both inside and out of the cabin, and the swatting and killing of these bloodsucking flying insects was the family's first priority, but it seemed for every one killed, two more took its place. The slaughter continued while Dora got the stove going and prepared supper. That night was spent hiding beneath the covers with the buzz of mosquitoes all around and waking in the morning to the scratching of welts left from their bites.

Late afternoon of the next day found them in Yellowstone Park, and though it was June, there was snow still on the ground, and the air was cold.

After finding a cabin that was open for the season, they repeated the procedure of the night before, but instead of mosquitoes, it was the cold. They sat huddled around a small stove with a plate of food on their laps, left over goulash from the night before, bread and butter, and a piece of cake with burnt sugar frosting and milk or coffee.

It was so cold they all decided to go to bed. There were two double beds in the cabin with canvases hanging from the ceiling to separate them, but once the beds were made up and everyone had crawled in under the covers, they were still freezing. Who would have thought it would be so cold in June to warrant warmer bedding?

Dora soon jumped out of bed and pulled the canvases from the ceiling. She laid one over each bed and climbed back beneath the covers. "Burr... it's so cold." She cuddled in closer to Ethel and reached an arm around little Mary cuddled close to Sam.

Alice, as nearly always, was in the middle between Luella and Edna in the other bed and glad for her spot on this occasion, or at least until they began to benefit from the warmth from the canvas.

In the morning, Sam got out of bed to feed the fire and put the coffee pot on to heat before going to the outhouse. Outside the cabin were large bear tracks in the snow and a short way off, he saw the bear lumbering off toward a patch of woods. He shuddered, remembering stories he'd heard of the damage a bear could do. Just the night before, another guest in one of the cabins had told him about a bear that had broken down a door at a place nearby when it was apparently searching for food. Sam had never encountered a bear before, and he couldn't remember ever hearing of them in Norway, but he knew there must have been bear there as well.

After a breakfast of bread and jam, they loaded the car and were on their way. Yellowstone had been a disappointment, but in later years, they would each see the beautiful grandeur of that magnificent park, and after all, the trip had been an adventure so far.

The roads, narrow and steep through the park and on west, were unfamiliar and frightening at times, so when they arrived on the outskirts of the town of Wenatchee, they drove into the first group of cabins they came to and paid for a night's stay. There was a toilet and washbasin in the cabin they were given, and they took turns taking sponge baths. The warm water coming from the faucet was an unexpected delight.

The food supply was running low, and Dora had seen a grocery store they passed only a short way back. Luella, Edna, and Alice anxiously volunteered to walk back to the store to buy what was needed. It had been a long while sitting in the car, and the walk would feel good.

The weather seemed much like it had in North Dakota when they'd left, sunny and warm, but the surroundings were vastly different. Instead of the open fields, there were grove after grove of trees planted in rows—some in bloom, some laden with unripened fruit, but when Sam inquired about the fruit trees, asking if that was the main crop there in the eastern part of Washington, he was told by the proprietor of the cabins, "Oh no. We grow a lot of wheat too. I hear you've fallen on some tough times in the Midwest, with the drought and all. I'm sure sorry to hear that since we rely a lot on rain as well and know how important it is."

Sam said, "Ya, it's been so dry, I haven't had a crop worth talking about for a long while, and this depression hasn't helped any."

The man asked, "Where you bound for?"

"Everett. I've got a sister there."

The girls returned from the store, and they all went in to eat. Seated around a small table, Dora asked, "Which way will we go from here?"

"I asked when I went to get gas about which way to go across the cascade mountain range, and the man who pumped my gas said to go by way of Blewet Pass. He said that that way we can hook up to Snoqualmie Pass. He said Snoqualmie is better than Stevens Pass. What do you think?" he asked Dora.

Studying the map, she said. "But Stevens Pass looks more direct."

"Ya, but the man said Stevens Pass is so narrow. Maybe we should go Blewet Pass?"

"All right. Whatever you think."

They left Wenatchee early the next morning, wanting to get to Everett by the afternoon.

As the road climbed, Sam remarked, "At least it's a good road, and not as narrow as some of the roads over the Rockies." But no sooner had he said that than just up ahead a man stood waving a red flag.

Dora said, "What in the world . . . he must want us to stop."

As they approached, Sam slowed to a stop, and rolling down his window, he asked the man what the problem was.

"There's a slide up ahead. It might take a while to clear."

As they waited, Luella noticed a stone drinking fountain at the side of the road.

"I'd like a drink of water, can we get out?"

"Go ahead . . . the man said it would be awhile."

They took turns at the fountain, enjoying the clear cold water when Edna went back to the car for her camera and took a picture of Ethel and Mary by the fountain.

After waiting some time, the man came over to the car and told Sam that he could continue on, so he started the car and started forward. The man shouted, "Take it slow!"

The warning was unnecessary because as they started to round the next bend, they could see a large part of the road was gone and all of their faces turned white as they sat like statues barely breathing. Sam's hands gripping the steering wheel and his foot barely on the gas pedal inched along the narrow edge of the roadway until he was well clear of the slide. Here he pulled to the side of the road, and leaning his head against the steering wheel, he breathed a sigh of relief, but it was a time before the color returned to his face.

The remainder of the trip was uneventful, and Snoqualmie Pass was a good road.

In Fall City, Dora looked at the map and said, "It isn't far now. Why don't we stop here and have a bite to eat and change our clothes?" She pointed to a gas station just ahead. "We can change our clothes in the bathroom at that gas station. We don't want to go to your sister looking like a bunch of ragamuffins."

Later as they drove down a street called Beverly Boulevard, they saw the house that had been described to them in Anna's last letter. A big house with a porch all across the front with stone pillars. Sam said, "Ya, that must be it, and he parked in front and got out and went up to the door and knocked, but no one came to the door, so he went back to the car, and they waited. In just a short time, Anna and Mildred came walking from the trolley stop a block away.

Sam recognized Anna immediately and hurriedly got out of the car. After they embraced, Sam introduced the family, starting with Dora.

After all the introductions, Anna apologized, "I'm sorry I wasn't home. I wasn't expecting you until tomorrow or the next day. Mildred and I went for a few things in town. Come in, you must be tired." Anna spoke with the same heavy Norwegian accent as Sam and their brothers.

After going in the house and getting seated at the table with coffee and a nice lunch of bread, ham, cheese, and pickled herring, and a plate of fattigmand, Mildred jokingly reminded them, "Don't forget . . . it was me who found you. Remember when I wrote to Ole?"

Sam and Dora laughed, remembering the letter that she'd addressed to Ole Berg, in Bluebells, South Dakota, and ended up in Bowbells, North Dakota, some months later.

Mildred soon excused herself. "I'm sorry, but I've got to be getting on home, Dave will be home from work soon." She was married to Dave Bradshaw, and they had a boy named Edward who everyone called Eddie.

The rest of the family would come to visit on Saturday.

Helen was the oldest, and she and her husband, Jergen Hansen, had a little girl named Marian.

Ester and Norman Kalanquin had two children, Fred and Delores.

Finn wasn't married, and Lucy who came after Mildred was married to Charles Wolven, and they had a little girl, Mary Louise, who was just a little older than Sam and Dora's Mary.

When Fritjof came home from work that evening, he'd already changed from his work clothes and washed up on the back porch before coming inside. He was a big gruff-looking man who greeted Sam and the family warmly. It was he who later that evening told the story of how they'd come to settle in Washington.

"I came to America in 1907, just three years after you, Sam. Your brothers Osten (Ed), Anton, and Ole had come a long time before I came, and even before you. You came in 1903 or '4, didn't you?"

Sam agreed saying, "1904! Your two oldest, Marit (Helen) and Astrid (Ester), were born, and I think you had another right about the time that I left Norway."

Fritjof went on, "Ya, that would be Finn. I think he was born in February before you left."

Anna broke in, "Nei, Finn was born in May!"

Fritjof scowled at Anna and went on, "I've never met Osten or Anton, but I think I met Ole once or twice before he came. Anyhow, I finally ended up in Eureka Montana and was doing good at farming when I sent for Anna and the children."

Anna broke in again, "Ya, I had the four children, but Helen and Ester were a big help. I'll never forget the name of that wooden boat, the Tiegen. It took us two weeks because of the fog and then I thought I lost one of my valises. A man offered to carry it, and then we got separated, but I finally got it back. Of course, I couldn't speak a word of English, and then the food I had along from Norway ran out, and the children were crying . . . and then we had to go from one train to another until we finally got to Eureka, and then had to walk near two miles. Uphill, all the way."

"Ya, but I met you, didn't I? And I brought some of the neighbors to carry the American trunk, and all those bundles and valises."

"Ya, I know, but there weren't so many."

"We stayed there in Eureka for a few years, and then we heard good things about Washington and decided to try it out and here we stayed. It rains a lot, but we like the trees and flowers and the summers are so nice, and it never gets so awful cold like the Midwest."

That night, Sam and Dora lay in bed and listened to the rain on the roof and talked of the dried-up fields at home, and how they'd hoped for the sound of rain that hadn't come. But then as they lay quietly, each in their own thoughts, Sam said, "We've been through some tough times, but this drought can't last forever, and then we'll go back home. It's nice country out here, but I know I'll miss the open plains and the clear air. I wonder if they ever get used to the smell of the pulp mills?"

When he finished talking, he looked over at Dora who was sound asleep.

Their time in Washington seemed to go by so quickly with all the visiting and sightseeing, but when the time came to leave, they'd made the decision to come back in the fall.

Sam had looked into the work situation and found it to be just as his sister Anna had said, and Dora agreed to move out to Washington for a time. She had told Sam, "We can bring Ma out to Washington too. I know she would really like all the greenery, and who knows, maybe Margaret and Ben and the kids will make a trip out and want to stay, and Luella and Charlie too."

In the meantime, Edna had found a job as housekeeper with a prominent family in Everett, the Gaiths who owned the bakery of the same name. This was a scary time for her, and she wasn't at all sure that she wanted to stay. It was true her family would be back in a few months, but without Luella, the sister with whom she'd always done everything, the one who shared her most special thoughts, but then she chided herself, remembering that whether here or there, Luella was now married and starting a new kind of life. It would be hard to be so far from Margaret too, even though she had already started a family of her own. She'd miss her and miss watching her nieces and nephews grow up. But in the wake of all these thoughts, she felt an excitement toward the future.

The day they left for home, Anna assured Dora that Edna would come home to them on the weekends, and that they would look out for her until their return in the fall.

* * *

The trip home to North Dakota was much less eventful than on the trip out to Washington, and it would be good to be home if only for a time.

Going the more northern route, they would stop in Montana to visit with Dora's brothers, Pete and Mil and their families.

Pete and Fay, by this time, had six children—Ellen, Walter, Hazel, Bud, Inez, and Laura.

Mil and May had no children of their own, but they had adopted Ellen's, Pete and Fay's oldest daughter's baby, because Ellen was very ill, and Mil and May so wanted a child. They named her Helen, and she was their only child.

One afternoon, Sam stopped for gas, and when he came back to the car after paying for the gas, Dora noticed a small bulge in his coat pocket and a big grin on his face and questioned, "What's in your pocket?"

He lifted a tiny brown-and-white puppy from his pocket and handed it to Dora, who said, "Oh, for heaven's sake," before nuzzling it to her cheek.

Alice and Lu were the next to hold the puppy, and then Ethel and Mary, until Dora took it back and named it Tricksey. A bed was made for her on the floor of the front seat, and Sam asked the station owner for a small container for milk. At first, the puppy didn't know what to do with the milk having been just taken away from its mother where it had nursed, but after Sam held its little mouth to the milk, it soon began to lick.

It was late evening by the time they pulled into the yard, and going past Mary's house, they saw that the lamps were already out. They would wait until morning to visit her and tell her all about the trip and of their plans to move, hoping that she would want to go with them to Washington. But in the morning, Dora found her mother sitting in her chair too weak to have even built a fire to heat water for her coffee.

"Ma! Are you sick?"

"Nei, just getting old, I guess."

"Have you seen Doc Hilts?"

"Nei. It's too far to walk, and I'll be fine. I must have a touch of something."

"Hasn't Mary Inga or Ella been in to see you?"

"Ja, but I was feeling fine then. Mary Inga wanted me to go home with her, but I said there was no need, and I like my own place. But how was your trip?"

Dora told her all about the trip as she got the fire going and made coffee and fixed a little breakfast, saving out the part about moving and then said, "I'll ask Doc Hilts to come over to see you. Is that all right?"

"Ja, it wouldn't hurt, I suppose," Mary agreed.

Dora knew she must feel bad to have agreed so readily.

It was soon learned that Mary's heart was not well, and she could no longer lie in her bed to sleep. When she did, she had trouble breathing, so sitting in her big chair with her feet propped up was the only somewhat comfortable solution.

When Mary was finally told about the move out to Washington and asked to come along, she quickly agreed. "Oh my, when will we go?"

It was Sam who said, "This fall. We thought September would be good."

"What about your house, and what will I do with mine?" she asked.

"We already have someone who wants to rent our house, and you can do the same if you want. Everything that we can't take with us will go in the barn, and there'll be room for some of your things too if you decide to rent your house. You wouldn't have to since you are not making payments, but we need the rent money to make our payments to the bank."

It was settled, and Mary's health seemed to improve in the excitement.

* * *

It was hot, with still no rain to speak of, and since they would not be there to harvest a garden, none was planted. Instead, Dora and the girls spent as much time as possible helping Margaret and Luella, while Sam worked long hours to earn the money needed for the trip back to Washington.

Margaret was soon to deliver her and Ben's fifth child and appreciated the help from her mother and sisters. One day as they carried water from a barrel hauled from Ben's mother's, Margaret asked, "Mom, what am I going to do when you go to Washington? You always make the krumkaker and fattigmand. I have Ben's mother's recipes, but it's not the same. And what about aebleskiver? I always have to borrow your aebleskiver pan. Ben's mother doesn't even know how to make them because they're Danish, but you can't have Christmas without them."

As Dora grinned and shook her head, she said, "Oh for heaven's sake! I'll write out the recipes for you and leave one of my aebleskiver pans with you. You can loan it to Luella when she needs it too. And you know, Christmas is a celebration of Jesus's birth whether there is krumkaker, fattigmand, or aebleskiver, or even lefsa or not."

"I know, Mom, but it's always been a part of our family's celebration."

"Ya, it has. I remember even when I was a little kid that Ma would save back sugar and the whitest of the lard. And she made sure there were enough eggs, especially for the krumkaker. It was the time above all others to celebrate. I don't know when the giving of presents came about."

"It must have been from when the Wise Men and shepherds brought gifts to Jesus."

"Yes, I suppose so, but it's always mystified me why we give presents to each other, but I suppose it's one of those traditions like lefsa and aebleskiver and all the rest."

The day baby Alice was born, Dora and Luella were there to help. Maude Barr who had delivered the others was in attendance as usual.

It was late when they heard the cry from the bedroom and knew the baby had arrived. Her name was Alice Eleanor Skredsvig.

Later, when Dora looked in on her daughter and the baby, she said, "She's a nice baby. I wish I could stay longer to help you, but Lu will, I'm sure. You take care of yourself."

Dora stayed on but a few days since there were things yet unfinished at home in preparation for their trip but before Sam came to get her. She'd written out the recipes Margaret wanted. She wrote the following:

Aebleskiver

2 cups of light cream, 1 cake yeast, 1 tablespoon sugar, 1 teaspoon salt, 2 cups flour, 2 eggs, well beaten, ¼ teaspoon cardamom, 1 cup flour.

Heat cream to lukewarm and add yeast and sugar. Wait until yeast foams and add the salt and flour and let rise two hours and add the rest of the ingredients and bake. Put one-half teaspoon fat in each cup of the hot aebleskiver pan, and add one good tablespoon of the batter and a teaspoon of cooked prune or apple. When ready turn, by using a tine of a fork and flipping it over to cook the other side, remove and cool. Before serving, roll in sugar.

Krumkaker

6eggs, 1 cup cool melted butter, 1 cup sugar, 1/2 teaspoon cardamom, and 1 ½ cups flour,.

Beat eggs well and add the sugar and butter. Add the flour and cardamom. Bake on the greased krumkaker iron over a hot fire. Use about one full teaspoon of batter for each krumkaker.

Hurry up and roll before it cools too much.

Mrs. Skredsvig makes better fattigmand than I do, so get her recipe. Just make sure your grease is hot enough to fry fast.

The following week, the week they had planned to leave, was frantic. Sam had to put the finishing touches to the trailer he'd built and get it loaded. While Dora cleaned the house for the people who were to rent it and pack last-minute things she'd nearly forgotten when Alice came running . . .

"Mom, it's Gamma, she can't breathe very good."

Dora dropped what she was doing and yelling to tell Sam she raced down the street to her mother's house. She'd already sent Alice for Doc Hilts. Running in, Dora sank to one knee by her mother's chair. "Ma, Ma . . . Doc Hilts is coming. Can't you breathe? Oh, Ma!"

Mary lifted a hand and placed it on Dora's and tried to reassure her, but Dora patted her and said, "Don't, Ma . . . don't try to talk."

Alice and Sam burst in, followed by Doc Hilts, and Mary was soon breathing better, but she was very weak.

The thought of Mary going to Washington with Sam and Dora was now out of the question.

Sam drew Dora aside and said, "We have to put off our trip. Your ma can't go and we can't leave her."

"I know. We'll just have to wait. Maybe we shouldn't go at all."

But a few days later, when Mary was feeling a bit better and she learned what Sam and Dora were planning, she called to Dora who was in her kitchen washing the dinner dishes.

"Dory . . ."

As Dora appeared in the doorway, Mary said, "Sit down! I want to talk to you."

Dora pulled a straight-backed chair up next to her mother and waited.

"Alice said you've decided not to go to Washington. Is that right?"

"Well . . ."

"Well, is it or isn't it?"

Dora explained. "Ma, Doc Hilts thinks the trip would be too much for you right now."

"Now listen here. I don't want you to be changing your plans on my account. You'll be coming back in the spring to get the rest of your things, and I'll go with you then. It'll only be six months . . ."

"But, Ma, I hate to leave you when you aren't feeling good."

Mary assured her. "Nei, don't worry, I'll be all right, and the spring will probably be better for me anyhow."

"We are going to wait until you're feeling better anyway, and won't you please go out to Mary Inga's or Ella's while we're gone? Or at least until you feel better?"

"Ya, I suppose I should."

When Dora told Sam what her mother had said, he went to see her. She, after all, was like a mother to him as well. Filling in for the dear mother he'd left in Norway.

"Ma, we'll go, but not for another week or until we know you're better. And you've got to promise that you'll go with us in the spring."

Mary assured him that she would. "No need to worry, and the spring will probably be better for me anyhow." And so it was all decided.

Sam loaded the trailer with as much of their household goods as it would carry, and on the fifth day of September, that year of 1936, they left North Dakota with Sam, Dora, and Ethel in the front seat, and Alice, Mary, and Tricksey, the little brown-and-white terrier, in the back.

They would return in the spring.

As Mary waited for Mary Inga and Charlie to come for her, she lifted the lid on what was still referred to as the American trunk and took the small leather-bound journal from its place and returned to her rocking chair.

It had been so long since she'd brought the journal up to date and turning to the last entry, she breathed. *Goodness, has it been so long?*

There were so many of the grandchildren and none of the great-grandchildren entered, and she penciled the names in their place.

Sitting back, she thought of John, "It's been twenty years since you died. I wish you could have known all those who were born after your passing, but by the grace of God, you'll all meet one day in heaven."

"Dora and Sam have left to find work in the state of Washington. Mill and May and little Helen are in Montana, and so are Pete and Fay and their family.

"It's only Mary Inga and Charlie and the youngsters, and Ella and Ole and their family left here of our children. Margaret and Ben and the kids are still here, and so are Luella and Charlie. Margaret and Ben just had their fifth child. I can hardly believe it."

Mary entered a few more things in the journal about the dry years and the Depression and how they had affected so many lives, and then she remembered that she hadn't wrote about Dora and Sam's house burning, so she wrote on.

The other day, I got to figuring how many babies I've watched come into this world, and I figured I must have delivered about fifty, give or take a few.

It bothers me sometimes that I can hardly remember the faces of those we left behind in Denmark, and yet I feel like it's only yesterday when we said good-bye.

I'll write more later on. Maybe after Sam and Dora come back in the spring.

She'd just put the journal away when she heard Mary Inga and Charlie's footsteps on the porch.

THE END

ABOUT THE AUTHOR

Mary Torbenson, an up and coming author with two published books and three more waiting in the wings. She has 4 grown children and 22 adored grandchildren. She and her husband make their home in the state of Washington.

CPSIA information can be obtained
at www.ICGtesting.com
Printed in the USA
FFHW021902130819
54302602-59974FF